The
What-If
Guy

Bree,
Miracles
Happen.
Love, Peace
+ Happiness

Taylor
Niki

The What-If Guy

Taylor G. Wilshire

NAUTILUS PRESS

LA JOLLA, CA

Published by Nautilus Press
Nautilus Press, a division of The Nautilus Works

This novel is a work of fiction. Names, characters, places and incidents are either the product of the author's imagination or, if real, are used fictitiously.

Special thanks to the Foundation of Inner Peace for granting permission to use excerpts from *A Course in Miracles*.

ISBN 10: 0-9778018-0-2
ISBN 13: 978-0-9778018-0-0

Library of Congress Control Number: 2006929481

Printed in the United States of America.

Cover by Greg Smith

Acknowledgments

Special thanks to Jeffrey A. Welch, Neva Sullaway, Eva Shaw, DeAnna LoCoco, Sylvie Rainsville, Deborah Myers, Chris R. Smith, Kirk Rees, David Hough, Theresa Heald, and all the many other friends that have supported me along the way.

But my greatest gratitude goes to my editor, Rachel Myers.

Chapter One

"Miracles occur naturally as expressions of love."

He saw me first.

I was leaving a sales appointment, and I was smiling. I had just closed a half-million dollar deal.

I passed him in the grand marble foyer of my client's building, a historical brownstone in Rochester, New York. Elegant sconces, most likely handcrafted in Italy or France, emitted a candlelight glow. Creamy walls sported oil paintings of European landscapes.

I remember looking back at him because his features were almost too handsome especially his sultry eyes. But I pretended I wasn't looking at him, more like I was looking through him.

He saw me.

He didn't look through me; he stared right at me. I felt the heat of his eyes and immediately felt awkward and uncomfortable. Despite my professional success and what my friends tell me are my good looks, my body sometimes feels like it belongs to a drunken puppeteer. I was caught in his gaze as if he had thrown a net over me which made me feel more clumsy than usual. I was worried that I'd likely trip or walk into a door if I wasn't careful. Story of my life.

The only times I don't feel out of place are when I'm immersed in work or hanging out with my two best friends, listening to music. I have none of the easy grace of my best friend, Sarah, or the sexy slink and swagger of my girl-friend Pam. Pam always laughs and tells me that I'm a hazard to myself because of what she calls my lean, strong and fast thoroughbred legs that operate like a newborn colt's. She tells me I have killer blue eyes and could land any guy I set my heart on. My heart wasn't set on anyone at the time. In fact, it had been more than a month since I'd gone out with anyone. Pathetic, according to Pam, and I had to agree.

But that day was different. That morning, I felt good, great, actually. When I walked across the shiny stone floor, the man's open stare told me that I looked good, and I believed him. I could feel his eyes drinking in my hair. I loved the fact that I could reach around and touch the ends in the middle of my back. By some miracle, everything was falling into place. Big things, like the deal I'd just made. Little things, such as the touch-up makeup job I did in my car before my meeting. It paid off. I had looked good for the client. I looked good for the stranger.

A sunbeam lit my path to the lobby door. My heels clicked on the marble floor as the palm of my hand brushed my lucky suit—navy, tailored, and expensive—which struck just the right balance between professional and hip. As I pushed the glass door open, I glanced back and saw his face. He was still staring at me.

I walked out that door well on my way to becoming a spoiled company sales rep. There was the President Circle trips and the company car, cell phone, BlackBerry, Palm Pilot, credit card, and supple leather briefcase with my mono-gram embossed in gold.

A banner year was ahead of me. I would again pull in six figures—an outrageous income for a person just out of college. I was on my way to becoming a millionaire before the age of thirty, or at least, that was my goal.

There in that lobby—with marble floors, museum-quality artwork, and a gorgeous man checking me out—I was pushing through the door into the sunlight of success.

—

Two weeks later I ran into him again. There was no mistaking that face, that body. And this time I noticed more—a tailored herringbone suit and no wedding ring.

He was walking out as I was coming into one of Rochester's more upscale properties, the Whyatt Building—imported travertine floors, fountains, and detailed craftsmanship that you would imagine seeing hundreds of years ago in Italy. Light music came from hidden speakers—jazz, nothing too complicated or stuffy but the type that is classy and sophisticated. The lighting brought out the highlights in his hair.

Judging by his grin, he'd just closed a deal of his own, and I was there hoping to close one of my largest accounts. I'd almost have suspected him of bringing me luck, but I had closed that deal on my own.

Three weeks later, there he was again. This was getting ridiculous. How many times can this Adonis land in front of me? He was waiting in another flawless lobby, this one of imported marble with furniture from an exclusive line in Paris.

This time I noticed how tall he was, maybe six-foot-three. He smiled, and I looked away as he began to speak.

"We have to stop meeting like this. They're gonna start calling us the tag team." He was confident and his voice was relaxed.

I couldn't help a crescent smile.

He fell into step beside me as I headed for the door and said in a charming and playful voice, "Hi, I'm Hank Larsen, Triangle Brokers." He stretched his hand toward mine as if to shake, but I missed his cue and instead reached for the door. I thought I left him in the lobby, but in a nanosecond, he was back beside me.

"I think we can help each other out." He craned his head, trying to get me to look at him.

Who was this guy? I turned and gave him a blank stare, too flustered to even be polite. "I'm sorry. I have to go." I stepped around him to head toward my car.

He continued, his voice deep and suave, his words well-rehearsed and flowing like thick velvet. "We're working on the same accounts. We should network."

Network? *Now* he had my interest. Could he tell how addicted to closing accounts I was? But I didn't lose my cool, and I tried not to look overly interested.

"I have some accounts that might be of interest to you. We could meet for lunch," he said.

I said nothing as I stepped into my brand-new company car.

He placed a hand on the door, leaned over and tried a new tactic in a playful voice, "I'm sorry, you said what time? Where?"

He made me smile. I was trying so hard to be composed. I reached for the handle and ended up closing the door in his face.

He knocked on the window. "Seriously you need to stop stalking me, it's embarrassing. How much longer are you going to keep this up?"

I pushed the button to let the window down but still couldn't find the words to say anything so he did, "Okay,

okay I got it already, stop begging. I'll see you at noon at Boyton's."

I gave him a face like *okay you win.*

I was grinning as I drove off, practically weightless. Unbelievable.

Down the street at the stoplight, I flipped open my phone to call my friend Pam. Voice mail. She was on her computer. I text-messaged her: "Gotta talk. Call cell."

Almost instantly, my phone rang—Pam was on the display.

"You won't believe this guy I just saw in the lobby," I said, panting like a Saint Bernard.

She laughed and said, "Stop drooling. You're gonna short out your phone. Divulge the details."

So I did, and she said, "Play it cool. Don't let him know that you think he's hot. Be engaging without being cocky, with a smear of aloof … mindful aloof."

Pam is my personal advice line. She can snag a man in seconds flat. We'd known each other since college. My friend Sarah hates her, probably because Sarah had finished her PhD, while Pam's ambition didn't extend beyond an "M-R-S." Pam was well on her way to graduating Phi Beta Kappa in the men department. I only wish her success with men would rub off on me. Well, maybe it had.

Friday couldn't come soon enough.

Chapter Two

"Fear binds the world. Forgiveness sets it free."

We met in the parking lot. The sun was in my eyes, which made me awkward and self-conscious as I walked up to him. Tongue-tied and not knowing what to do, I stretched my arm out and gave a too-firm, sweaty handshake, and then handed him a business card.

He looked down at the card. "Ryley McKenna. I thought you wouldn't show."

"Yeah" was all I managed to say.

We walked into the restaurant. Everything was magnified. Each step I made across the lobby floor echoed in my ears, as adrenaline poured through every vein. The lighting was faint, and the place was packed with suits. My eyes adjusted and I began to get my bearings; the chemistry between Hank and me was thick. I tried to sneak a quick look at him but was slowed down by his hair. My eyes, marveling at the shine, remained there, and I wondered what it smelled like. I looked too long and walked into a chair occupied by a businessman taking his first bite of a burger. "Oh, I'm so sorry!" I said, mortified. Still chewing, he nodded as if to say, "It's OK."

"Don't be a goofball," Pam's voice rang in my ears. "Make it about business and stay cool. Remember the business and don't be a klutz."

What I had learned in the business of sales is that it didn't matter what you were selling—phone systems, office space, or pencils. The key was getting people to talk to you. Networking was key. No one likes to cold-call; you need a good introduction to take the cold out of the call. The referral was the key to getting in and closing business without the arduous effort of calling someone who doesn't know you and convincing that person that he or she wants to.

So we got down to the business at hand.

His hands were large, beautiful. He leafed through a small black daily planner (I had brought whole files, folders, and my Palm Pilot). Surprisingly, there were few entries in Hank's planner, just a scribble or two on each page. He glanced at the few words on each page and revealed names of businesses and contacts, phone numbers, and e-mail addresses. All that information gleaned from one word in his planner. It wasn't a planner; it was a prop. Everything was in his head—amazing.

I couldn't write fast enough. I looked up from time to time and followed the round of his sexy lips and admired his straight teeth; he must have worn a retainer as a kid. That nose. A perfectly sculpted nose—big … WASP-y big. He was a classic hunk.

Hank said, "These accounts are complete lay-downs."

"I'm sorry, what?"

"You know, they're ready to sign. They're moving because they are expanding—they'll need to upgrade or get new phones. I'll let them know you'll be calling."

The phrase, "complete lay-downs" swirled in my head as I looked outside; I had chosen the seat facing the window. Pam said I should always sit where the light catches my eyes, making them look their bluest. She also told me, "When you meet a guy, always look detached, not standoffish, and don't act like a goof." I had to work on the "not like a goof" part, especially when I found myself playing nervously with my earrings.

The restaurant tables were crammed together, and the voices melded into a monotonous buzz, punctuated by an occasional piece of cutlery scraping a plate. Glasses rattled, and chair legs scratched and screeched on the hardwood floor. A skinny woman's irritating, high-pitched laugh reached top decibels, while Hank projected the ultimate in playboy cool. He had on a tailored, pinstriped, gray suit that looked expensive, with a tie that was designer-gone-bad—all the colors made me dizzy—but somehow he pulled it off.

I wore a classic khaki suit with a silk scarf that Pam showed me how to tie. When she tied it, it looked sophisticated. When I tied it, it looked like a knot. That day, it looked like I was strangled by a knot. My favorite tasseled loafers with the low heels were to stop me from tripping in front of him, and on my ears were my lucky silver-ball earrings that I couldn't keep my hands off of.

When the food came, I had a hard time looking at Hank—his beam was too high. It's not like I'd never been around good-looking guys before. It's just that this guy was big time, smooth and out of my league.

I realized salad was a very bad choice because the lettuce wasn't cut up and the veggies were the size of small farm animals. Every time I took a bite, some verdant surprise bulged out of my cheeks, making me look like a squirrel with too many nuts. I was afraid to say anything for fear of a carrot chunk hitting him in the face.

So I smiled a lot and made *hmmm* sounds, nodding with overstuffed cheeks. When a small dab of salad dressing oozed from the right corner of my mouth, I reached for an extra napkin and my elbow connected with my water glass. Ice scattered to the floor as a river of water cascaded into my lap, cooling down any thoughts of a romantic lunch. But Hank handed me his napkin, discreetly signaled for the waiter, and smiled to let me know it was no big deal.

Once the salad was cleared from the table, I was able to speak a little more freely. Hank directed the flow of conversation. I was reserved and businesslike, trying to recover from my salad fiasco. He volunteered that he wasn't married and lived in a prominent downtown neighborhood in a six-bedroom mini-mansion. I wondered how old he was but speculated that he was only a year or two older than me. He definitely was pulling in the mega-commissions.

When lunch was over, I walked away with three prospective deals that could close before the month's end. Hank walked me through the parking lot. As we approached my car, he lightly touched my elbow and leaned over to say something. The chemistry was too much—my limbs melted and oxygen left my brain. He let go of my elbow, I'm sure because of my gaping mouth.

"I was wondering if we could meet for drinks."

How could he be asking me out? Didn't he notice that my skirt looked like I was a candidate for Depends? He misread my confused look and silence for a no.

"We could go over deals."

The paralysis was too much.

"You know," he kept trying, "get more business for one another."

"When were you thinking?" The words came out sounding more professional than I expected.

"Tonight."

"Oh, I don't think so."

"I know you probably have other plans, but you should

try to break them. I'm meeting a group of brokers from work. It's actually perfect for you." And then the smile that could melt polar ice caps.

All I could do was nod.

"There'll be one or two of our brokers and a partner. These guys are loaded with contacts. Hey, you'd be missing a lot of good business." That smile again.

I smiled back as I slipped into my car.

"Right, that's what I was thinking. But a guy can dream can't he?" His face flushed and then added, "We'll be at the Wall Street Grill. If you feel uncomfortable, bring a girl-friend."

As I opened my mouth to decline, he placed his hand over mine, and suddenly I felt like a small girl, star-struck with one touch.

"Just think about it."

"OK, I will," I said nonchalantly.

It had been close to a month since I had been on a date, and being twenty-something, that month felt like a lifetime. I didn't want him to know about my present dry spell. Another tip from Pam: "Guys want girls that other guys want—being too available can make him think there's something wrong with you."

I doubted that Pam could come on such short notice. And Sarah wouldn't want to go—bars were not her thing. But I had to meet him again. I had to. Only I had to do it without seeming as if I wanted anything more than those deals he kept dangling in front of me.

Back in the car, I called Pam. She picked up on the first ring. I gave her the scoop. She was at work, so she whispered, "Oh, Rye, I can't go out tonight. I already have plans. Come on—it's Friday!"

"Yeah, I know, but I had to try."

Silence. She didn't have to say anything. I knew she would if she could.

She then added, "But scope them out for me! If Chip Nichols is there, say hi!" Click.

Then I called Sarah. I was desperate and in need of reinforcement. "You have to meet me at the Java House," I demanded. The Java House was a trendy coffe shop where we escaped the day-to-day.

"When?"

"Now."

"Are you on drugs? I can't leave the lab." Sarah's work was always so damn important. Well, actually it was. She worked for a bioengineering and pharmaceutical firm that was looking for a cure for AIDS, cancer, multi-strand viruses, and about a million other scourges of the human race. No matter how many damn times she told me what the hell she did, I still had no clue. I mean, I knew she was a scientist and a bioengineer. It was the rest that I had a problem with. I'd always tell people, "She studies tsetse flies and genetics to find the cure for multi-strand viruses," which isn't exactly right. It infuriates her, but in all the time we've known each other, I don't think Sarah and I have ever been mad at each other for longer than an hour.

"You have to. It's serious."

She groaned. I could picture those tiny hands running through her light brown bob, always straight and perfect, just like her teeth.

"All right. Half an hour. That's it."

"Perfect." Now all I had to do was persuade her to go to happy hour with me.

The first time I saw Sarah Toadvine—"Toad," in middle school—I knew she was cool. Super-cool. Not because she had all the right clothes and accessories, or amazing hair, or even because she was breathtakingly beautiful. It was the way she observed people that made her so cool.

She watched people with such assurance and authority and gave off such confidence that I was immediately drawn in. I had never met anyone, let alone a preteen, with that much poise.

She's been through a lot, but she always remains centered and calm. It remains my favorite quality about her to this day.

And another thing—it's hard to believe that she's only five-foot-two and weighs nothing. She fools you when you look at her; you could swear she's at least five-foot-nine. Was it her independence or the freedom that she had as a teen, or the intelligence that got her into Harvard before she turned seventeen that duped you? Was it her ability to speak articulately and with serene assurance?

No. It's the way she can look at you and know immediately who you are. She says it's an old-soul thing.

She got me that first day I saw her, and I got her too.

And even though she could have picked anyone, even the most popular girls at school and probably the most popular girls on the planet, she picked me. She picked me to be her best friend, and I am a better person because of it.

Sarah was sitting in the back of the Java House with her latte and my decaf mocha, no whip. I suddenly realized I'd barely eaten at lunch with Hank. I was starved.

"What's up?"

"I need a blueberry scone!"

She rolled her eyes, impatient to get back to finding a cure for Alzheimer's.

"OK." I scooted my chair to the table. "Here's the thing:

I need you to go out to the Wall Street with me at six-thirty. The guy I met at lunch wants me to meet him there with his friends." I knew I was pushing it.

"You mean tonight … with what's-his-name?"

"Hank."

"Hello, Ryley, it's me, Sarah—remember me? I'm not going to a bar, especially a meat market like that. Besides, I have prana tonight!" Prana meditation classes. I completely forgot, another woo-woo metaphysical specialty. How could I ever keep up with all her weird classes?

"Come on, Sarah, I'd do it for you."

"I'd never ask you to."

"Please, you don't understand. What if? What if … I mean … you know? You have to see him. You have to. Then you'll know."

"Rye, the guy's a player. What do you know about him, really? I bet you a million dollars he looks good, didn't know your name when you met him at lunch, and hangs out with guys who are named Chip, Sloane, or Scooter." She took a swig of her latté and looked at me with that look that I hate—the intuition-on-hyper-drive look. "I bet he rates 'chicks' before he meets them and bets with his buddies on how fast he can get them in the sack."

She was starting to piss me off. "It's not like that, Sarah; it's about business."

"C'mon … the only business he's interested in is the business of you naked."

"Toad, I really want you to meet him. And what if he's the one?" She rolled her eyes. "What about all the synchronicity? We keep running into each other."

"You don't need me to tell you he's the one. Besides, I don't like him already," she said, packing up to go.

"You mean you're not going?"

"Ryley, not only am I not going, I can't even understand why you would even ask."

"Because you're my friend, and you believe in soul mates."

Sarah knew everything there was to know about the human soul; she was the authority on anything spiritual. I knew I was pushing it but still had to try.

"OK, already, I got it … I just need you tonight, that's all," I said.

"You know, what you need, Ryley," she said, rummaging through her bag, "is this." Sarah took out a paperback that could have fooled you for a dictionary. It was navy blue with a strange title, *A Course in Miracles*.

"They teach a course in this?"

"It's about the power of love and forgiveness and the notion that with that, everything is possible." She then pushed the book at me as she slung her leather shoulder bag across her back.

"Are you saying I need a miracle? Or it would take a miracle to find my soul mate?"

"It's a course on letting go of fear and replacing it with love."

"What are you talking about?"

"It's a course in training your mind. Its emphasis is on application versus theory, or better yet, experience rather than theology."

"You should hear yourself."

"Let me make it simple." She cleared her throat and spoke quietly. "It's about letting go of all our anxieties, old baggage that gives us a feeling of lack, and replacing that emptiness with love, in all places of our life—professional and personal."

"Oh … my … God. You're serious," I said, shaking my

head. Then after a deep breath, I said, "If I take it, will you go?"

Her look gave me the answer, so I handed it back to her. I never would've read it anyway.

I went to the office and wrapped things up—went through e-mail, voice mail, got things ready for my early appointment on Monday. As I was leaving the office, I thought about Sarah's book.

It was a good thing I'd given it back to her. I couldn't imagine what it would be like to be caught carrying that around. I went home to primp for the night and wished she would show. But I knew better.

Chapter Three

"I trust my brothers, who are one with me."

It was drizzling as I approached the cobblestone-and-brick pub. Car tires hissed along the wet street. English ivy clung to every rock of the building, exposing roots and veins. Inside, beyond the leaded-glass windows, the light shone warm, illuminating a dense tangle of suits. Happy hour was well underway when I arrived. I was dreading the possibility that I would meet these men alone and that the rain would make my hair frizz, and their first impression would be "Nice girl, but what is that stuff on her head?" First stop: the ladies room.

As I stepped into the smoke-filled bar, the warmth of the room hit my cold cheeks, making me flush. The warmth came from the many glowing fireplaces and all the hot suits smashed together without enough breathing space. The place was packed. It was my first time there, so I had no idea where anything was, such as the restroom.

The building was two stories, dating in the late 1800s. It had a traditional, conservative feel—hunting pictures, mahogany, and brass everywhere. It felt like a men's club; for all I knew, there could be a boar's head on the wall behind me or maybe a moose.

I was three steps inside when I saw Hank waving me over to his group of Wall Street look-alike executives—all handsome, all well groomed. I wanted to go to the bath-room to check what I looked like.

Little did I know what I was walking into.

I hesitated as I approached the group. Like a gentleman, Hank graciously stood up and made the introductions. I greeted everyone with a professional handshake and then pretended to look around for my girlfriend, who was now breathing through her groin as she meditated.

"Yeah, she's … um … about five-foot-two; short, light-brown hair; pretty. Seen her?" They all said no, so I excused myself to go look for her—in the ladies room.

After pushing and squeezing my way through the bodies that were standing and sitting everywhere, I made it to the overcrowded restroom.

The smell of perfume lingered thick. The line was ten women deep. Finally making it to the mirror, I was relieved to see that the rain hadn't made me look freakish. Surprise. My hair, makeup, suit, and bladder were fine. I typed out a plea on the tiny key pad of my phone to beg Pam for any last-minute coaching. "What to do when you are alone with a bunch of Wall Street executive types and you want to act cool but feel very nervous. Pam, are you there?" No answer, so I headed back.

Arriving back at the table of men, I mumbled, "I couldn't find her."

Hank offered me a martini. I swallowed hard and said, "Sure, how about a Grey Goose?" It was a drink our division manager drank—I'd never had a martini in my life but wanted to fit in.

I scoured the room for happy hour munchies. There had to be something in my stomach besides a blueberry scone if I was going to drink with a bunch of professional fish. There were two dried-up chicken tacos in a stainless chafing dish on a table by one of the fireplaces. The last of the leftovers from happy hour. I walked casually to the table with my back to the group of men and inhaled both. Then I daintily placed a few carrot sticks and a dab of blue cheese on a white plate.

I swallowed hard, feeling the tortilla carve a hole in my esophagus as I spun around and headed back to the table. Hank handed me a drink, and I took a large sip to wash the tacos down. The martinis continued to flow like Niagara Falls.

The boys were laughing and carrying on, and it was easy to toss in an occasional witty remark. Hank was to my left; we were at a table by a fireplace and adjacent to the martini bar. Before Hank introduced me to the guy on my right, I spotted Chip—Pam's Chip—across the table. I smiled a hello and then began talking business to the guy to my right. I overheard from across the table, "Dude, that girl's checking you out." I nonchalantly looked to see who was talking— Chip and his friend. "Which one?" the friend said. "She's with the group over there," Chip said, gesturing with his eyes.

"Nice rig," the friend responded. They didn't know I was eavesdropping; I was typing in leads from the guy next to me on my Palm Pilot.

As the guy next to me continued to talk, I casually noticed one of the partners across from me—tall, dark, and married. He began to flirt with a slinky blonde with heaving cleavage, got a good peek at her chest, and then poof, his wedding ring mysteriously vanished into thin air. All that remained was a ghost of a tan line.

Hank then introduced me to a handsome guy who had been scoping for his friend to his left. He nodded toward me and then looked around as he made a toast to Grey

Goose. A shy smile revealed his beautiful mouth and dimples to a brunette, who was now next to the blonde with the big boobs. That smile was his calling card, and it reeled in the babes. He leaned into Hank, and I overheard him say, "Dude, check out the blue top," referring to the new brunette.

Meanwhile, I continued to ply Hank's friends for leads, and they were more than obliging. Hank's boys nodded with approval as though I were just initiated into their fraternity. They liked my witty remarks, my business savvy, and that I laughed in all the right places. "Ryley, give Alex Winton a call at Liberty Financial. Tell him Rex sent you." My fingers worked at lightning speed to get in the goods. They cordially joked that I must have grown up on vodka and olives.

Incoming. The ladies were swooping in. Not the trashy, slutty types—these were the women who went to school for "MRS" degrees, or at least their mothers did and had taught them well how to catch good money-making stock. The brunette had about as much experience as I did with martinis, but she had less common sense. I felt for her. She took the bait and three sips later, she was drunk. She went after the brooding, wounded frat boy next to the married guy—dark hair, dark eyes, and dangerous. She was the sweet, nice type; I could tell by her comfortable shoes. I wanted to caution her.

I wanted to her to clear away from this bad boy. Danger, danger! Too late. She began flirting full out and messily. I overheard him say, "Listen, we're just having a guys' night out. I don't want to hurt your feelings, but I just want to hang out with the boys tonight." She didn't get that he was teasing, and he started to laugh. "I'm joking, darling. What's your name?"

I couldn't hear what she said.

When the pairing started to square off and when a

wardrobe malfunction exposed the nipple of the large-breasted blonde, it was time to go.

I thought I was doing OK until I stood up. That's when I had to really get out of there, and fast. The room was a vortex, and I could tell that I was about to see the tacos again. I rushed to the front door for air, holding back surging gags. Just as the cool, night air started to settle the spinning world, Hank came out.

"Hey, th … there," I said, as if he couldn't tell I was blitzed.

"What are you doing out here?"

"Oh … I … thought …" I waved a hand, and even I could see how exaggerated the movement was. "I thought I saw my friend. But no thuch luck. Gotta get going." The tacos were advancing upward.

"No, stay."

"Would you do me a favor? Could you go get my keys? Left them. Can't fight that crowd." I waved toward the bar as I tried to sound normal. "Please." I put my hand on his arm and felt that familiar surge warming my palm.

"Sure."

All I could do was smile for fear that he would be wearing something new on his bad tie.

Finally, after what felt like eternity, he went inside to retrieve my keys, which were actually on me, inside my purse. And I ducked into the bushes and lost my tacos. I wiped my face and felt for anything leftover.

Feeling much better, I carefully walked toward the parking lot. The air felt like liquid Jell-O as I wove closer to my car. The sound of running wingtip's closed in on me. It was Hank, doing the five-hundred-yard dash. He must have run track in high school.

"Hey, where you going? I couldn't find your keys."

I waved them in the air to show him I had "found" them. I had to concentrate on every syllable. "Home."

"Why?"

Where was that button on my key? Not the red one! Damn, how do you turn that horn off? He pointed toward the ignition. At last, contact, engine started, obnoxious horn stopped, people went back into the barn. I mean bar. Double-vision kicks in. Where is that eye patch I keep in the glove department?

I want to tell him that I had a nice time and got a ton of business but didn't want him to smell vomit or hear another incoherent word come out of my mouth. So I shut the door all too forcefully and waved good-bye.

My idiotic, stubborn ego drove me home. Beyond stupid. I should have called Sarah, or a cab. I could have killed someone, or myself. Thank God—for God and all his friends, like angels and their friends, guides, masters, the universe—for getting me home safely. I was still thanking every single creature, large and small, fat and skinny, dumb and smart, when I hit the pillow.

The unfortunate curse: I didn't drink a drop of water or take a single Tylenol before I passed out in bed.

Chapter Four

*"Miracles are seen in light, and light and strength
are one."*

I woke up to the hideous blaring of my telephone.

I muttered a prayer, pleading, begging that it would stop. "Hail Mary, full of grace …"

It didn't, and I found myself crawling to the phone, still fully clothed from the night before. My bra was killing me; I could feel the deep impression where the underwire had smashed the thin flesh under my breasts straight through to my rib cage. I rubbed the dark-pink railroad tracks it had left there, as I made my way out of the bedroom.

My stocking feet made it easy to slide over the polished hardwood floors as I headed for the small table where the death-screeching instrument laid. As I picked up the receiver, I immediately sprawled onto the Turkish rug. With eyes closed and deep concentration on breathing, I prayed again: "Please make the room stop throbbing, and could you send some oxygen to my brain?"

"Hello," Death said; I mean, I said.

"Ryley?"

"Yeah." Who the hell could be calling at this hour? "What time's it?"

"Hey, it's Hank. Uh, ten-thirty."

My head was filled with cobwebs and my tongue was

stuck in mud. Oh, my God, it's Hank! Shit! Now what? Tongue, start moving!

"Just called to see if you made it in all right. After you left, we closed down the martini bar."

"You did?" I said, rubbing my forehead. Spiders were breeding on the cobwebs in my mouth. My throat was drier than Hades.

The pounding in my skull tore at my brain cells. The amount of alcohol I must have consumed had certainly killed off critical neurons, no doubt the ones acquired from birth to kindergarten—the years of language development.

He was speaking: "And how about the boys? They didn't offend you, did they?"

"Gumy phone num?" I blurted.

"Oh, you're listed." His clear, smooth voice revealed not a trace of a hangover, and he could translate drunk. How nice for him.

"Yeah," I said, as I began to slide across the living room on my back, pushing the floor with the balls of my feet as if I were rowing my body like a scull. My crewing method was not foolproof: My toe snagged the edge of the rug sending the small table, which held the base to the phone, crashing. As I continued to crew to the kitchen, my suit jacket began to jam in my armpits. My skirt was soon a wad around my lower rib cage. My objective was to get to the fridge to get something to drink and *not* to lift my head. I didn't want to topple over. Who was the inventor of the cordless phone anyway? Complete genius. God, without the cordless phone, I'm sure I would have been a complete mess.

After slithering into the kitchen and waiting a short eternity to gain strength, I collected enough courage to lift myself to my knees. I searched the inside of the almost-empty refrigerator. One of the few traces of sustenance was a carton of milk I had bought the day before. The creamy liquid gushed down my throat. I poured too quickly or maybe guzzled too slowly, and milk flowed over the sides of my mouth, hitting the lapels of my jacket. The suit was heading for the dry cleaner's anyway. The liquid was cold and wet, and I hoped it would renew my brain.

That's when I realized the phone had gone silent. Hank was waiting for an answer.

"Could you say that again?

"I had no idea you'd lived in Ireland."

Oh, God. I sifted through our conversation from the night before. What had I said? Had I spoken in an Irish accent? In college I lived in Ireland for three months, trying to find my ancestral roots—my way of finding where my father's heart lived, seeing that it rarely lived with us. The only thing that brought him closer to me was the beer that I brought back with me.

The phone fell silent again.

"Do you think we could get together?" Why did I say that? I wanted to take it back. I meant to ask if I could call him back.

"Sure, when?" he asked.

"I don't know."

"Give me directions."

Chapter Five

"The power of decision is my own."

When I hung up the phone, I couldn't believe I'd just given him my address. I justified my forwardness because technically, I had known him for more than a month. I mean, I did see him for the first time six weeks prior, and I'd thought about him every day in between, and after all, he did ask me out for lunch and drinks. He didn't seem like a psycho.

I crawled to the bathroom to survey the damage: a swollen face with slits for eyes, a chalky complexion, and severe bed head stared back at me. I had no time to dry my hair, so I had to shower quickly and do the ponytail number.

Just as I stepped out of the shower, the phone rang. It was Pam. "So how was it? Any my types?" Not even a hello. No need.

"How was your night?" I asked, shaking the wet out of my hair with a towel.

"Bust. Went out with this group set-up thing ... people from work. You know, 'Oh Pammie, you gotta meet this guy. He's perfect for you.' Yeah, right—complete loser."

"Drag," I said, throwing my suit in the closet.

"Yeah, I should have gone out with you. How was it?"

"A drunken mess. Hey, what's good for a martini hang-over?"

"Bromo-Seltzer!"

"I don't have any," I said, back in the bathroom.

"Then three Tylenol and one or two gallons of water and a bunch of eyedrops." I grabbed the Tylenol and headed for the fridge for bottled water. "So, any my types?" she asked again, with a strained and impatient tone.

"Actually, yes, there was one geeky guy, with glasses, who looked as smart and sensitive as you."

"Really?" She tried to be natural, but her sarcasm came through.

"Yes, but he's married and didn't go to Wellesley."

"It's too bad; I could have lived with the married part. Who was there?"

"God, I can't remember all their names. Rex Smyter, Jack somebody ...."

"Nope, nope."

"Alex Wint ... or Winst ... something. "

"Sounds familiar."

"Oh, yeah, your friend Chip Nichols."

"Chip Nichols! Oh, it was a night of pretty boys!"

"Well, actually, yes, but I gotta ton of business. Really a ton!"

"Are you sure? Chip's a friend, but those are the types of guys who have gotten away with the best of life because of their looks, not 'cause they do their homework."

"No, really, they were OK—regular guys."

I gave her the lowdown as I put on makeup with hands that trembled like a heroin addict's.

When the doorbell rang, I'd downed the Tylenol, chucked down a bucket of water, and was finishing peeing, having barely just put on a pair of khakis—I really needed ten more minutes.

I threw on a white turtleneck, green cotton sweater, and a pair of green loafers, no socks. I shoved the tail of the turtleneck down in the back of my pants, said good-bye to Pam, took a deep breath, and opened the door.

God, he looked great. His hair freshly clean, cleft chin showing through the perfect amount of stubble, and cheeks rosy from the crisp fall air. He wore a preppy fisherman's sweater, jeans that made his ass look out of this world, and a pair of worn driving moccasins. His boys had called him "the bank" last night, like he was always in the money. Sarah would not have approved.

"Hi ... you look great," he said with a dimpled grin.

He kissed me on the cheek. My vision blurred, then slowly steadied ... steadied ... and was back.

Like a perfect gentleman, he opened his car door for me. Once inside, my mind went absolutely blank; he probably thought I was stupid. It was just stage fright. I used "I'm a little hung over" as my excuse when he asked why I was so quiet. His confidence was mesmerizing but not contagious. He made me cautious of every word; it was like figuring out what I was going to say for an acceptance speech for some big, prestigious award. Not that I would know; I mean, outside of President's Circle. But I'm sure if I did get one, I'd go to the podium frozen and end up saying nothing I'd hope to say, if I even managed a feeble thanks before falling off the podium.

He took me to the newest deal-closing restaurant, retro but not noisy, expensive—a top-three eatery with class. It was right on the canal. Ducks and wild geese were still swimming in the water, despite the autumn cold. The restaurant was in a converted warehouse and painted sage with near-black trim. Inside, there were chrome accents and a fire pit in the lobby; the interior was sophisticated but not stuffy. Whimsical light fixtures in cobalt blue and lots of indistinct glass sculptures adorned the space.

That's where I fell in love with Hank.

Like magic my self-consciousness melted, warmed by his charisma and confidence. We talked about everything—and nothing—as I ate a two-ton tuna melt and a mound of French fries. I was starved. "Nice appetite," he said, without judgment.

"Well, you know." I was embarrassed, but I couldn't help my raging hunger—anything to get rid of my hangover.

After lunch he gently took my hand and said, "I want you to see something." I hoped my hand wouldn't get sweaty. I felt like I was turning into a puddle with his touch.

He drove an enormous Range Rover. It was a Y-chromosome car all the way—rugged, a little beat up on the outside, dirt marks and scrapes, and a few bumps. It had done some manly things.

The difference between Hank's car and mine was that my car was my second office, while the inside of Hank's looked like a normal car. His car was minimalist by comparison. Leather seats, vacuumed, CDs neatly in their cases. My car was new but overflowed with stuff. Sarah called it my mobile home—or cesspool—depending on her mood.

First, there was the work stuff: a small filing cabinet was wedged between the seats on the back floor. It was filled with technical manuals, network flowcharts, the *Wall Street Journal*, and business magazines, in case I needed something to read in between appointments. There was always lots of extra paperwork, too—contracts and contract supplements like MOUs (memorandums of understanding), equipment profiles, customer profile sheets, notepads, anything that might be needed on a call. There was the just-in-case personal items: gym clothes, sneakers, both tennis rackets and lots of extra tennis balls, a swimsuit and towel, and of course, in the glove compartment, tampons. And then there were the survival items—bottled water, PowerBars, Motrin. You never know what you might find. There could be a left-over sandwich from the day before, or a still-unwrapped birthday present, or a bag of cleaning supplies and paper towels that hadn't made their way inside my house. If I got into an accident, I would probably be killed by flying debris inside my car, not by the impact outside.

Hank took me to the middle of nowhere, the sticks, where streets were no longer wide. To the right, in a thickly wooded area with golden- and red-leafed trees tightly packed together, was a dirt path. As we came upon it, Hank spun the Rover, entering the narrow road that was the width of a hiking trail. The car was moving too fast, my lungs were stuck in my throat, too much speed for a girl with a hangover and two tons of tuna barely in her.

Hank had that bad-boy grin.

The Rover cut a path through small trees and coarse shrubs. Tree branches scraped the sides of the car as the massive metal vehicle bobbed and tipped. The motions were sharp and scary, like a roller coaster minus the rails. What the hell was this guy up to? Can I trust a guy who kills me on a first date?

We careened down a muddy eighteen-foot cliff. As the car dipped and dragged through boulders and shrubs, my toes were pressed so firmly into the carpet that I felt like I was thirteen, back in ballet class en pointe. It was too fast. Hank's face, however, assured me that he had done this before and lived to tell about it.

Out of nowhere, a breathtaking view of the countryside spread out forever. Hank pulled to a stop and sprang around the Rover to help me out.

"You wanna walk?"

So now he was the Marlboro man. He stretched his long

legs and walked in front of me, leaping like a mountain goat from rock to stump to path. I tried to keep up, but my motor skills were still on martini time. Did he drink last night?

"Watch out for those branches," he said, as a pricker bush thrashed back and got stuck in my hair. He turned around, smiling. "You're going to love this."

I already did. In that moment, I felt a heat oozing down my throat to my chest, and butterflies danced in my heart. A "bliss-out"—calm and excited at the same time. The crimson red of the autumn leaves, the rich scent of pine, and the maples so bright and yellow. The colors of the landscape seemed to have been turned up a notch or two. And standing in front of me was Hank, his smile just for me.

Chapter Six

"Light and joy and peace abide in me."

The view from the edge of that field made me feel small. The land had an energy that made me wonder if American Indians had performed their sacred ceremonies on the spot right before us in times past. The colors of autumn had made their way to the birch and maple, as well as to the shrubs—pitch pine and scrub oak. Brilliant oranges, golds, and ambers with ruby reds radiated through every leaf on the property, which extended for miles. In the summer there would've been tall grass where we stood; it had turned into wheat-like stubble. Is it possible to be nostalgic for a place you've never seen before?

Hank walked toward a collection of boulders the size of coffee tables. I stumbled and tried to look casual. His eyes politely averted as I clumsily fell and then made a seat for myself.

"Not bad, huh?" He grinned again as he settled gracefully on a gray, speckled boulder beside me.

"Yeah."

He told me the story of when he'd first found this property. Triangle Brokers was looking for a new site to build on. They decided not to buy this untouched land.

Sitting with his right knee drawn up to his chest and

arms loosely wrapped around his shin, he slowly turned his head toward me and asked, "So, who's Ryley McKenna?"

"I don't know." I felt too nervous to really answer and wanted to be the one asking the questions. "You first."

Looking right into my eyes, he said, "On the outside I'm gangster rap … but inside, I'm Mozart." He smiled; he was kidding.

I burst out laughing. "Are you from here?"

He smiled. "Nope." Then he shifted his gaze to the fields in front of us. "I was born in Lake Forest, Illinois." He looked over to see if I knew it. I didn't. "It's old money, and we didn't have as much as most. Dad's a doctor; Mom stayed home with my sister and me. Let's see … we went to private schools, and then I went to Duke and graduated in finance. Most of my friends are loaded. I'm not, but working hard to be so one day. I like to work out—anything cardio, like basketball. Love this out here." He looked right at me. "OK, what about you?"

I stared back like a deer in headlights; all the ease I'd felt in the restaurant was gone. "What about me?" Yikes, what could I say?

"Where did you grow up?"

"Here."

Silence.

I tried to think of something, anything, and then stammered, "Do you like what you're doing?"

"You mean Triangle?"

"Yeah."

"If I really think about it, there's never been a place I'd wipe off my slate. It's the people that I play with that I like the most; it doesn't feel like work." He continued speaking slowly and gently. "I like the freedom of sales." He was looking at me—really looking at me.

"Me, too. Are you still friends with the kids you grew up with?"

"Nah. My friends are stuck doing the same things they were doing two years ago, while my career is skyrocketing."

"Do you go back?"

"Yeah, to see the parents, and my sister lives in Chicago. We don't see each other much."

I wondered about that. How could you lose touch with your family? Sure, mine drives me nuts, but no way.

He saw my face and said, "These are the business-building years."

I wanted him to go on but didn't want it to be so obvious that I had nothing to say. I could tell he was getting anxious for me to say something, anything, about myself. So I changed the subject to music and books and was pleasantly surprised that he took the bait. Our bookshelves and CD holders carried the same stock. He loved Bryan Ferry, Pinheads, and even more, loved the same songs—there's something about loving the same song; seems almost tele-pathic.

I asked him what he'd be doing in five years and kicked myself after it came rolling out of my lips because I was starting to sound like I was interviewing him for a job.

"I can't even tell you what I'll be doing in five months, but I'd like to say that I'd still be closing multimillion-dollar deals and knocking down a deal that would put me on the cover of *Commercial Real Estate* magazine."

I thought I was the only one who wanted to be on the cover of a business magazine.

"Maybe settle down and bring my wife breakfast in bed. The truth is I don't feel like I need to know what the future will bring. I like the ride."

"You cook?"

"Love it."

"No kidding," I said, as I leaned back on my elbows and wondered if this guy was for real.

"Do you play tennis?"

"I play OK."

I knew if we ever played, he would be so much better than me. This was a guy who would be good at anything.

Out of the blue, without a drop of preparation, he asked, "Where does your heart go when you're alone?"

"Home," I said, without knowing how or why.

"Where's home?

"On the coast of Maine, picking blueberries. Where does your heart go when you're alone?"

He wouldn't answer. Instead, "Why Maine?"

"It's where my family would spend our summers. It was heaven."

"Really?"

"It's the only place where I didn't feel pressure from my dad. It's the only place I didn't feel like a failure. My Dad's third-generation Harvard and has high expectations. I seem to never live up to them. I didn't get into any Ivy League schools, so I went to the University of Rochester for business and never finished my MBA. I was in the three-two program—undergrad in three and then grad in two—but I just couldn't pass the fourth year. Education is big in my family, really big. Not to mention my being the first not to go to an Ivy League in four generations. You know it really doesn't matter about IQs or degrees anyway; common sense is what's important, right? Well, my sister went to Brown and my brother went to Harvard, so you know who the favorites are. I like the outdoors too, but prefer tennis over anything. I hate tattoos and body piercing and manicures. I think counting calories is a waste of time."

Could I please shut up? His question ripped me open, surprised me. Words I hadn't been able to find flooded out. I tried to switch gears and lighten up but was frozen. There I was, exposed, naked, and dumb. I was mortified that he would think that I was some kind of moron.

He leaned into my shoulder where I could feel the warmth of his breath. "You know, competition can make you lonely … but it doesn't have to." He must have sensed my awkwardness and landed me back on earth, straight from hell.

"I haven't told you, but I cry," he said with a perfectly straight face. Was he for real? "Yeah, I watch chick flicks … and I would be lying if I told you I didn't cry," he said with a sarcastic grin. I laughed.

Even though I was holding back details about my driving force, it felt good to let someone know about my family, even if it was a small piece. The only person who knew the whole story about my family was Sarah. She knew all the real secrets, and I knew hers.

As I lay back in the coarse grass, still laughing, with the sun heavy in the sky, Hank leaned over and kissed me, first gently on my cheek and then softly on my lips. He was warm and yummy, too good to be true. But here he was; here we were. In that moment, time stood still and I was in heaven. As I opened my eyes, I felt connected to more than the land that I rested on; I felt like I was connected to everything.

The day slipped away while we sat on the hill that overlooked the world. It was a perfect day. As we opened up to one another more and more, I found my voice again. We laughed together and swapped stories and shared the little secrets that bring people close. He exposed the stuff that guys don't like to share, the stuff that makes them real and approachable.

When it was time to go home, he hinted that he wanted

35

to go home with me. His openness made me feel close to him; I wanted to get even closer. But I knew better than to move too quickly.

I told him I was tired. "But if you want, stop over tomorrow."

When I walked in the door that night, my first thought was to call Pam, but the phone rang before I had a chance.

"Hello?"

"Hey ..."

"Toad?"

"Where've you been? I've been calling all day. I had the court for one o'clock!"

Sarah and I played a lot of tennis as kids and still do when we can. It was her mother's idea, years ago, to get Sarah into tennis; still hard to believe. Sarah's mother didn't play tennis, or watch tennis on television, or even like tennis. It's hard to understand what she did like ... well, except cigarettes—chain-smoking and vodka martinis. Her mom was always out of it, out of touch. It's not like she ever forgot to pick Sarah up from school, or take her places, like tennis lessons. Actually, from the outside, her mom looked like the perfect, responsible mom—hair pulled back with a hair band or ribbon that matched her outfits. Always present at school functions. But she really wasn't present. I didn't get that part 'til much later in our lives, but looking back, it was clear all along.

"Oh, my God! I forgot! He came over."

"You slut!" she said teasingly.

"No, no, it's not like that! We did brunch and a hike and ... and ..."

"Slow down. You can tell me."

But I really couldn't. I couldn't tell her too much guy stuff. "OK." Deep breath. "We drank martinis at Wall Street—"

"What? Who is this?"

"I know! Can you believe it? So I go to Wall Street *alone*—"

"Yeah, so?"

"And I meet his buddies and two partners. By the way, how was breathing in through your ass last night?"

"It's not breathing through your ass! It's meditation and pulling up the Mother Earth energy into your chakras. It's very grounding."

"Oh, so *she* was breathing up your ass."

"Ha-ha. So tell me more about last night and what's-his-name."

"Hank."

"Yes, Hank."

I told Sarah the events of the evening but left a lot out. Sarah can be prickly about some things, and that makes her judgmental. At least I felt judged. Pam would get the good stuff—like how remarkable and amazing Hank was, and how I felt like I was really falling for this guy. I could give her all the goods.

But Sarah only gets the Cliffs Notes. And when I gave them to her, she didn't say much, which said it all. She never came out and said or even hinted that she didn't like or trust Hank. But I knew her all too well. She was being too damn nice.

"I'm so glad, Rye. It sounds like you had a great time. He sounds perfect. Can we hit the courts tomorrow or do you have another date?"

"Well ..."

"OK, call me when you come up for air."

Damn. She really did hate him.

"Well, what about you? What are you up to?"

"I got a bunch of reading I want to catch up on. Mom's cooking beef Wellington, I might stop over. Charlie's going over. I'm playing it loose this weekend." Her brother Charlie was about to pledge a fraternity.

"OK." I wanted her to like Hank. I wanted to stay on the phone.

"Bye, Rye!"

I let her go and let her polite opinions be. "Bye, Toad."

I usually trust Sarah's intuition on my life as a whole, minus the guy stuff. But maybe she had it all wrong about Hank. I'd have to figure out how to get them together, because I knew she'd like him if they met. After all, what's not to like about a guy who can cook?

Chapter Seven

"Nothing real can be threatened. Nothing unreal exists."

I checked the messages on my cell after I brushed my teeth, right before Hank arrived.

"Ryley, this is your dad. I haven't heard from you. Have you finished filling out the applications? I'd like to know when you plan on finishing your master's. I can—"

Delete.

Next message, my sister: "Oh, Rye, you are not going to believe it. They are publishing my dissertation. Can you believe it?" Yes, I can, I said to myself. "Not the one on my first PhD; the one on social interaction on human—"

Oh. please. *Delete, delete.* I tossed the phone on the couch.

When Hank arrived, he made himself comfortable in my living room—my favorite room in my first house. It had hardwood floors trimmed with nine-inch baseboards, original to the hundred-plus-year-old brownstone. The walls were painted a beige-like "desert fawn," highlighted with white-gloss crown molding. The wide-planked birch floors were covered by three oriental rugs from my parents' house, the few things I was able to snag from home. The furnishings were modest. Under the only painting I owned, an old landscape by an unknown Dutch painter, sat a navy sleeper sofa heaped with blue-and-white down pillows, patterned like old-fashioned ceramics. Two white pillows bordered with navy piping and centered with my monogram framed the ensemble.

Completing the room were two matching navy blue director's chairs, a wing chair with a slipcover of brightly colored geometric flowers, and a lobster-trap coffee table from Maine. There were three floor-to-ceiling bookshelves filled with everything that I'd kept since kindergarten. And lastly, two handcrafted decoy ducks from Maine, one perched on top of the lobster trap and the other on a bookshelf.

I was spacing out, trying not to think about the message I had just deleted, when Hank pulled me back. I thought he was talking about politics and was too embarrassed to admit I hadn't been listening. "I think we are in a time of deliberate lying and cruelty."

"Stop reading the paper. That feeling will pass," I answered, as I handed him a glass of water.

"Seriously, people don't listen," he continued. "I told this guy at work what he needed to do and he blew the deal anyway. If people would just listen to me … I mean, come on, I've excelled in everything I've done. I know what I'm talking about."

I wasn't listening to his words. My eyes were on his face. At that moment he had such a deep sorrow behind his eyes. "What happened to you that makes your eyes so sad?"

He started to blurt out something, but he suddenly seemed guarded, got up, and began pacing. I could tell he really wanted to tell me. I found out later it wasn't like him to be so sensitive so early on in his game.

Then he sat down in one of my director's chairs and reached into the breast pocket of his bomber jacket. "I have something for you." He pulled out a CD. Bryan Ferry. The music is dark, haunting stuff with a rumbling of romance.

"Get out of here!"

"Track five's the best. *Windswept.*"

As I flipped over the CD to read the back, I found a bright red-and-yellow leaf tucked into the case, a personalized CD cover. A leaf from yesterday's spot.

"You made this."

"Nah."

He invited me to sit on his lap. With my legs dangling over the armchair and his ring finger outlining the details of my face, he said, "I gotta tell you something." His face was serious. His palm slowly and gently cupped my chin. "Here's the thing ..."

My face was open. I let him speak.

"Over a year ago, I moved here from Illinois; this girl came with me. It's not working. We live in the same house but not in the same bedroom. We're just friends." He paused. "She's moving out. It's just taking time for her to find a place."

I studied his face for a moment and could see that he was telling me the truth. He looked as if he were caught in a bad place, stuck and frustrated. Was that what the sadness was about? It didn't seem like such a big deal.

He continued softly, "The first day I saw you, I knew I'd see you again, and when I did ... I couldn't stop thinking of you."

"Really?"

He raised his eyebrows and with a playful grin said, "I thought you were a ten."

I gulped down a laugh. This would definitely not be reported to Sarah.

He caressed my knees and carried me to the sofa, where we unraveled the events of the day, and then he said, "This is fun and everything, but why do you still have your clothes on?" I laughed, and with a serious face, he added, "I can't rub your feet with all your clothes on."

I smiled, he smiled, and he kissed me, but my clothes stayed on while we made out.

The days grew into weeks, and fall turned into winter. Each day became short, bleak, and cold, with not much snow but lots of wind and ice. You could find us at my house or out for a meal at the nicest restaurants, drinking martinis at Wall Street, hooking up for lunch between appointments.

He mostly came over.

Our relationship deepened, changing from dating to sleeping together on a work night. I was two steps into my home from a grueling day at the office, with not even my coat off, when the phone rang. I cupped my hands to breathe in warmth. It was Hank.

"Can I come over?"

"Sure."

My movements weren't fast enough. I tidied every room—picking up shoes, smelly workout clothes, magazines, library books, and PowerBar wrappers—and washed the dishes. To an untrained eye, the place looked spotless, but I knew there were dust monkeys hiding under more than the bed. I placed lit candles everywhere—chunky candles, tapers, tea lights, votives. No spot was spared. Even though the place was a fire hazard, the colors warmed and gently softened.

After stepping out of a hot shower, I looked through my closet for something sexy. I slipped on a black, cocktail-length, sleeveless silk sheath with spaghetti straps, and dressed it down with bare feet. A quick dab of perfume went under my chin, ears, lower stomach, and in the crook behind both knees. My hair dried on its own and curled naturally. Later, I would loosely wrap it in a matching silk hair tie.

Hank's CD reached the end and started over. It had been well over an hour since his call. He was taking too long—I was ready.

I went from sitting in one chair to another, picked my cuticles on my left hand, trimmed both big toenails, and rearranged books on my bookshelf until I saw a tattered, green book of novenas—Catholic prayers in paperback.

I wasn't a practicing Catholic but liked novenas. They are formal, repetitious prayers that are said over a finite period of time, like a mantra that states an intention again and again, until God takes over. My thoughts were nonstop requests: "Please, God, have Hank show up"; "Show up safely"; "God, please make him the right guy for me."

After another half hour passed, I gave up praying. "Where the fuck are you?" I said out loud, looking outside into the darkness.

In the kitchen, over a glass of milk, I went back to praying for a small eternity, and still no Hank. I took the small book in the palm of my hand and rubbed it against my chin; I could barely smell the pages. I inhaled it deeply and exhaled slowly. I thought about Hank. I thought about our relationship, and I asked myself what exactly it was that I wanted— what I wanted in my life on the whole, not just the present. My mind moved slowly and methodically.

Sure, there was the success I'd set my heart on, my father's approval, but even more, I wanted a fairytale ending. I took a deep breath, exhaled through my nose, sank deep within my heart, and realized I wanted more than for Hank to show up. I wanted my knight in shining armor.

My dream was to have a relationship with a man who

would allow me to be the best that I could be, someone who could be a safe place when I physically, mentally, emotionally, or spiritually couldn't do life on my own. I would be the same for him. It didn't have to be a perfect match or a soul mate, just someone real, someone really good for me. I hoped it would be Hank.

I must have repeated the novena a hundred times. "Hail Mary, full of grace, thou art with me. Heaven and earth, I come in the name of the Lord, Hosanna in the highest. Grant me peace ...." The period of time was now heightened to maybe a millionfold. Then, finally, I let the prayer rise into the heavens and nestle in the clouds over my head.

Another hour later, Hank walked through the door. Still in his dark suit from work, he sauntered toward me and scooped me up in his enormous arms.

"Hi, where—" I tried to say.

He cupped his hand over my mouth and pushed me against the wall.

"Sh-h-h ... take your clothes off."

He sank his mouth into the soft part of my neck, then chin, and up to my mouth, as he pushed me harder and harder against the wall. I drew in the scent of his skin, flesh, and breath. My fingers clung to his jacket as I buried my mouth in his hair. Soon, my ankles were wrapped around the small of his back, as he kissed me deep and long, until all I could do was moan.

Slowly and carefully, he stepped us away from the wall. Our bodies entangled, a mesh of heat, and just as I realized where he was stepping, it was too late.

We were on the floor, taken down by the only oriental rug without a pad. As we fell, we knocked over a candle on the corner of the lobster-trap coffee table. It flickered out. Hank, strong and agile as ever, managed to fall without hurting either of us. I burst out laughing. "Bet you meant to do that!" The only injury was the candle wax on his suit pants, which he'd have to explain later.

Unabashed, he carried me to the bedroom. I felt so light. He laid me down and slid his hands backward over my face. He moved from business suit to birthday suit. When he took off his shirt, I was blinded by his stomach—homegrown muscle. My God!

I let out a whisper. "How do you stay so fit?"

"I got a trainer who kills me."

More like a mad scientist.

His touch turned tender, and we made love, over and over. Skin on skin, flesh on flesh. It was the kind of lovemaking that made me wish I were a smoker because when we were done, I wanted a whole pack.

The mood of the night was annihilated at 3:37 AM, when Hank got up to leave. We still had the glow of sex, and I wanted his arms around me to spoon. Why did he have to go?

Something inside me felt close to not deserving the frosting on the cake. I wondered if Hank's housemate, Elizabett, had more significance than he admitted, or maybe I was paranoid. He was ruthless in the way he talked about her—never anything good or right about her—but she was still there living in his house. Was he hiding something? I was too chicken to ask.

I craved his words and wanted to believe them. "I can't get enough of you. I've never met anyone like you. I love you." Never having had an affair of any type before, I didn't know what to expect. I rationalized that it wasn't a real affair, because he wasn't married. I wanted to be his one and only. I just couldn't come across as needy, so I never asked.

I never asked when our nights were halted abruptly before 4:00 AM. I never asked why he never invited me to his house. I never asked why we never double-dated with his best friends, because I knew the answer and told myself it was what it was.

Sarah, on the other hand, had something to ask or say. The silent disapproval I'd been sensing had come out into the open after the first night Hank and I slept together, and she wouldn't let up.

"So where did you guys go last night?"

"He came over."

"Really." I said nothing in response, so she continued on. "He's a player, Rye. Be careful."

"You don't know him. You don't how soft he is in the middle."

"Maybe you shouldn't be so attached."

"What the hell does that mean?"

"You know. Don't get too heavy."

I took a deep breath. "You gotta get over your crap about men." Giving advice was always heavy on her agenda. She always wanted to prove a point, defend me against her fears. Why couldn't she let up and just be glad that I'd finally found someone to love?

"You're right, you're right, I'll stay out of it." She shut up for all of a minute and shifted to her Zen-like state of awareness. "All I'm trying to say is that real love is already inside of you, the love that lives inside your heart that you were born with. You know your essence. You don't need to find things or people outside of yourself to make you feel whole. Everything that you need that makes you feel perfect, whole, and complete lives within you because that's where God is—inside your heart." She paused because she knew I wasn't buying it. "You're right, Rye. Let's change the subject. You want to come with me to yoga on Wednesday? It's so relaxing. You'll find a moment of peace. We can go out to dinner after."

There was a time when Toad's giggle would send me howling, like when we were at her apartment when I was a freshman in high school. She had her own apartment because she went to the University of Rochester when she should have been a sophomore at high school. She transferred to Harvard a year later.

It was so cool to have a friend my age with so much freedom. She could do anything she wanted, even when I had to be back home by nine. We'd eat popcorn and watch movies and she would giggle that great giggle, and I would start laughing, and then, all of a sudden, I was snorting the popcorn because I was laughing so hard, which would make her laugh. And then I would be choking, and she would be giving me a fake Heimlich and then … we couldn't contain ourselves. We were laughing and snorting and couldn't even remember why or how it started.

But then I got older and realized she was really alone, even though I thought I was with her. She was really alone, and I wondered how her mother could expose her to that kind of danger, leaving her on her own at such a tender age.

Chapter Eight

"Miracles transcend the body."

At the office, I was overwhelmed with work: customer appointments, proposals, service orders, product meetings, conference calls, internal meetings, and phone call upon phone call. There were a gazillion e-mails and voice mails; accounts were closing left and right, and there were problems, like an install not going well or a legal dilemma with a contract. It was endless. I was checking my wireless constantly. I might get three or four urgent messages in a meeting. There were nonstop interruptions. But then a good one came from Pam: "Did you have Hank on Rye last night, or Hank with a cherry on top?"

I instant messaged her back: "I can't get him out of my head."

"It's early in the game. Play it safe."

"But I don't know if it's real. I'm confused about what's really going on."

"Completely normal."

"So what do I do?"

"Play one day at a time, and don't overanalyze. You're fine. It's fine. He's fine."

"OK, fine … how are you?

"I'm double-dating with Chip Nichols tonight."

"Good luck."

"Ciao."

I didn't tell her about the conversation I had the night before. I'd asked Hank if he wanted to go away sometime, and he stunned me with his non-answer. "I don't know … we're different, that's all. It's always the thing that you think won't happen that does."

"What?"

And then it was if he were changing the subject. "I'm really different from my family. I woke up today and realized if you can't go backward, try working with what you got. I'm gonna spend more time with them." He was letting me in, letting me in close.

But then I wondered if he was really talking about them. I was obsessing, thinking about what he had said, replaying it, and trying to remember every word and nuance.

Even when I was in a meeting, closing a contract that day, I was thinking about our conversation, not the business at hand. I tried to focus on the work but couldn't. New business was churning for me at the office. The contracts couldn't be written up fast enough. It was as if my phone number was on the bathroom wall of opportunity. Surviving in the office was like skiing moguls. If I could pull my legs underneath me when I hit a bump and control my momentum and speed, I'd make it.

Even though work was crazy, I found myself drifting off, remembering the way Hank washed his face in my bathroom. I'd be on the phone, talking to a customer, and in mid-sentence I had no idea what I was talking about. As I was writing up the paperwork to new orders—stuff like spreadsheets of network designs—Hank's smile would pop up in my head, distracting me from the task at hand. And even though his voice resonated deep and slow in a spot inside my heart, there was a lump of uncertainty that stung my throat. Something didn't seem right.

I left that meeting still thinking about the night before. Hank had been talking about his family: "You know, my dad really wanted me to go to law school. It killed me to let him down, but I had to do what I wanted. I'm happier for it, I think. Fear of failure motivates me, too, maybe too much. Or maybe it's unconditional acceptance from my parents. You don't get anywhere in life without learning from them."

I found myself staring blankly at my cubicle wall, seeing nothing at all, as I went deep inside, asking myself where this relationship was going. I was manic. My eyes were glued to the gray fabric on the wall as I wondered who he really loved. Was our relationship meant to be? Was this real or a figment of my imagination? Was he my novena? I needed immediate confirmation.

So, for the first time in my life, I did the unthinkable. I went to a psychic. Insanity makes one do strange things.

I knew Sarah would know the best psychic. When I asked her, she responded with, "You want what? You're kidding, right? This is *so* not you."

"I can't help it. I'm going nuts."

"Wow, I guess so."

Sarah handed me a ratty-edged card from the depths of her wallet.

I didn't believe in psychics; I thought they were a bunch of quacks. Who would waste money on them? My church suggested that psychics practiced black magic, maybe even devil worship. I thought the church had a point.

"Maybe this isn't a good idea," I said, my senses coming back to me.

But Sarah would not let this good fortune go. "What's

wrong with you, Rye? Get out of the Dark Ages. They don't ride brooms! Channeling is a form of communicating—a direct line from God!" Sarah's voice became gentle. "I'm telling you, Rye, the psychic's excellent and she can help. Have I ever steered you wrong?"

The truth is, Sarah has never led me to anything but good.

The day I visited Sarah's psychic, I was more than nervous—anxious, worried, edgy, and panicky was more like it. The air was colder than dry ice and the winter ground was frozen hard. After parking my car in her driveway, I headed toward the house, looking around as if bats were about to attack me. Or maybe I'd get mauled by a black cat hiding in the bushes. I managed to make it to the front of her house in one piece.

When I reached the doorstep of the small, suburban house, she opened the door—and looked surprisingly like a normal person. She didn't look satanic or witchlike. She looked like someone's mother, short and a little frumpy, with a neon-pink, flowered apron. Her name was Fran.

She was drying her hands on the bottom of her apron when I noticed how round she was, like a perfect marshmallow that plumps up over a campfire. "Oh, come in, dear," she said as she led me to the kitchen in the back of the house. She spoke with a milk-and-cookies tone; I immediately relaxed.

Even though I was comfortable, I made sure not to reveal anything about myself. Not one single hint. She probably thought I was rude because I made noises instead of officially speaking. "Can I get you something to drink, dear?"

"Unh-uh."

I wanted to see if she could give me insights into my situation without a clue from me. I wanted the good stuff, answers that would make me say, "Wow, how did you do that?" I did not want to hear something someone makes up because she wants you to feel good about yourself. I needed something authentic.

After laying out her cards, she leaned over the table, her stomach squishing in. "You have a love interest presently in your life." I said nothing but thought, *Doesn't everyone, on some level?* No real mystery. She hadn't made a point yet.

"You have spent many lifetimes together."

"What do you mean, 'lifetimes'?"

"You're soul mates."

I looked at her with a scrutinizing eye.

"We have many soul mates in our lives; this man goes back a long way."

"What do you mean?"

"During the Renaissance, you were married to each other and very in love."

"What?"

This woman was nuts. Strange, prickly goose bumps made their way down my arms and up my spine. I tried to ignore them. The information was bizarre and eerie—yet familiar. I couldn't allow her to convince me that such an extravagant idea was real. I didn't even believe in reincarnation. The images of the past lives she described, however, were intimate and peculiar and strangely convincing.

She described a manor, where we supposedly lived, centuries before—the massive stone hallways with tapestries, the fields where we went riding. Part of me believed that she was playing a creative game. But another part believed her.

She continued with the reading, flipping strange cards with Japanese-like pictures. The cards were much larger than playing cards but easily and comfortably fit in her small hands.

"You'll be moving out West—California."

"Huh? No, no." I had absolute no intention or any interest in ever moving out West, especially not California—the land of fruits and nuts.

"Soon, with someone you love, but you will not spend the rest of your life with him," she said, ignoring my remarks.

"What do you mean, 'soon'?"

"Within a year."

She was dead wrong. Her transmitter must be jammed. California? I'd never even seen it.

What was so interesting was the fact that she described my family perfectly. She nailed my dad's occupation and pegged my mother's eyes and wavy hair. I guess it couldn't have been too hard because we look so much alike. She also scored on the brother and sister and where I fell in the food chain. When we were through with the reading, Fran leaned over the table and looked hard at me with penetrating eyes. "You have the gift of manifesting miracles."

"Excuse me?"

"We are all capable. You have the gift. Here … take this."

There it was again.

She handed me the same blue book Sarah had tried to give me; it felt like a five-pound bag of flour. The book was paperback; its cover was tattered and worn. Inside there were nearly 1,200 pages. The title on the cover was written in heavy gold block letters. Some of the gilded letters had a dull gleam, and others were missing edges. As I peeked inside, I noticed the pages were transparently thin and were fragile and delicate to the touch. The book was titled *A Course in Miracles.*

As I leafed through the thin pages, I wondered why this

strange book had been given to me, twice. Was there something to it? What on earth did Fran mean by manifesting miracles? There was something intriguing, familiar, and even flattering about the notion. Was it magic? What nonsense! Nevertheless, I had to look. I gingerly opened the worn cover and thumbed my way to the introduction:

This is a course in miracles. It is a required course. Only the time you take for it is voluntary. The course does not aim at teaching the meaning of love, for that is beyond what can be taught. It does aim, however, at removing the blocks to the awareness of love's presence, which is your inheritance. The opposite of love is fear, but what is all-encompassing can have no opposite. There is no order of difficulty in miracles. One is not "harder" or "bigger" than another. They are all the same. All expressions of love are maximal. Miracles are everyone's right.

I had a miracle in mind.

Chapter Nine

"Miracles are natural signs of forgiveness."

After leaving Fran, I couldn't wait to tell Hank about our having past lives together. What a concept. I wanted to discuss what that meant for the here and now.

It was Saturday, and Hank had called about two to say he was on his way over. The sun was still high in the sky, which made tree shadows dance on the hardwood floor of my living room. We hadn't seen each other in two days because of our hectic work schedules. It felt like a lifetime.

When he called, he'd said, "I'll be right over. I have a surprise." I couldn't wait.

Time stood still, like watching cold water come to a boil. I felt like a hamster on its wheel, spinning but going nowhere. I moved about anxiously, accomplishing nothing: couldn't read a magazine, couldn't finish washing the dishes. I attempted to make my bed but flopped on top of it instead. Then I went to my closet and got dressed and changed my clothes. After I was dressed, still no Hank. I went back to try on something else, picking one outfit after another, but ended up with the original—white turtleneck and worn jeans with my navy loafers, no socks.

I lit a candle and said a small prayer but very, very loudly. "Please, bring Hank quickly!"

Minutes slowly dribbled by, a half hour, then an hour,

then three hours. Still no sign of him. The sun was starting to set, making the shadows on my floor turn into darkness. Out of boredom and anxious anticipation, I pulled on a coat and went outside to sit on the porch swing. It was an old bench swing suspended by thick, prickly rope. I let my legs dangle, with my hands tucked under my thighs, warming them. My mind raced. Dangerous thoughts of a mangled body in a car accident, firemen putting out flames—my mind surged. I felt sick.

Two painstaking hours later and still no sign of him, I called his cell phone for the fifth time. It was still turned off. I walked through every room of my two-bedroom house a million times: upstairs, downstairs, on the porch, inside, outside, inside, upstairs, on the bed, downstairs, on the couch.

I frantically looked out the window, obsessed with his arrival. My eyes fell on the lobster-trap table and *A Course in Miracles*, still where I had left it after my visit with Fran.

I picked up the book and placed it on my lap, closed my eyes, and took three slow, deep breaths. My arms relaxed and my body began to slow down. I let my shoulders soften as I said aloud, "Please, God, give me an answer."

I opened the book at random: Lesson 18, *Workbook for Students*.

"I am not alone in experiencing the effects of my seeing …"

I nestled on my couch, sinking deeper and deeper, not holding on to anything. Half-past nine, the phone rang. I was relieved to hear his voice.

"I got in an accident."

"Oh, my God!" My heart stopped.

He continued. "I was picking up one of Elizabett's cigarette butts on the floor and … someone rear-ended me. I just can't deal with you right now."

Deal with *me*? Ouch.

His breathing was unnatural, like he didn't want anyone to hear him in the next room. "I was going to surprise you. I was bringing over the '57 Porsche convertible. I knew you'd love it. Then, bam—it was like a sign. I just can't deal with this …."

"What do you mean?" I asked.

"I don't think I should come over. I think we should slow things down … it was a sign."

Silence. I was taking it like a spoonful of wasabi with no soy sauce. "Why do you keep saying that?"

"I just think it was."

I was numb. He was supposed to come over. What was I hearing? What the hell was he saying? I'd just found out that we were soul mates, and then God, or the universe, tells him not to come over and gives him a sign. Something was really screwed up. What kind of god gave such bad advice?

I let go of the phone after he hung up. I was hurt, spent, crushed. My heart felt scraped out with a butter knife.

Thoughts of a soul mate flashed before my eyes—tag-teaming accounts, passion in the bedroom, walks, dinner, and hanging out in my small living room. I was dying inside, melting into sadness.

I needed help. I called Toad.

"Jesus, what time is it, Rye?" It was only ten at night, but she always goes to bed early so she can meditate before dawn.

"This is a crisis. Time doesn't matter!"

"What happened?"

After filling her in on every aspect, point, detail, and fact, I let out a breath and asked, "What am I going to do? I was just starting to believe in something ... in something good ..."

"You mean past lives?" she asked in a sleepy voice.

"No! In Hank."

"Yeah, I meant Hank."

I began to sob. "I'm broken in a million pieces. What did I do wrong?"

She interrupted. "Maybe it wasn't meant to be."

"Toad!"

She was quiet. I let it out. "I can't believe he said that ... 'I can't deal with you.' Do you know how many times he said he loved me? He told me he hated her. And then cigarette butts! He gets signs from cigarette butts? What the hell was that? What was he thinking? I hate him so much right now. Am I a body without feelings?"

"Absolutely not! You had the courage to open your heart and love, and sometimes love stinks. Rye, you are beautiful inside and out. You didn't deserve this and you didn't do anything to cause it. You know, sometimes life just hands us lessons that are hard, and this is hard, but it doesn't mean that you are not bigger than it or that you can't get through it ... Rye, listen to me. I believe within us is a light that radiates greater than a million suns. We are born with it and it is our essence, but we forget that it's there and we forget how powerful it is. That light is you."

She was making me feel better. She could have said I told you so, but she didn't. She was just there for me with the right words, like a proper toast. In a proper toast the attention is on someone other than yourself. You never turn the spotlight on yourself. It's brief and kind and inspires affection.

"You want me to come over? You OK?"

"No, I feel better. Thanks, Toad."

"No problem. Are you sure you don't want me to come over?"

"Sorry. No, go back to bed. Love you."

"Love you, too."

With superhuman strength, I walked to the coffee table and picked up *A Course in Miracles.*

I am not a victim of the world I see.

I threw the book across the room.

There was no way I was going to bed; I was going straight over to Hank's house—for the first time. I knew the address; I had lifted it off an envelope in his car more than a month ago. My heartbeat was thick and heavy in my throat, throbbing faster than a jackrabbit's.

I slowly drove by once and then circled and parked under a tree four houses from his. And when it was the perfect time, when I could be sure that no one noticed, I strolled over as if I were taking a midnight walk. But my stroll turned Rambo when I ditched into his front shrubs beneath a bay window. Slowly, carefully, I poked my head up to take a peek, and there before my eyes was Hank. No, not right in front of me. He was in the hallway walking toward her, toward Elizabett. And in that moment, I realized how wrong I had been about the whole thing.

This was not the bitchy, stand-offish, fat, unsexy woman that Hank had painted. She was tall, blonde, with a pleasant face, even pretty, and she really looked nice, like I could be friends with her. Nice, like we could have drinks and laugh out loud. She was not that horrible, mouthy, mean person he talked about. He walked up to her and softly hugged her, tenderly, gently, like he does to me—like he *did* to me. He was so warm and sweet, and she was the same with him. And in that moment, I was crushed—my aorta sliced in two.

Here was the guy who could have any woman he wanted, and he wanted all of them at the same time. It wasn't fair. I felt so weak; my tears blurred my vision, and a thorny shrub pulled on my shirt, leaving scratches. But I made it out of there and made it home, where I lay awake, my mind racing, despite the heaviness that made me so tired.

ℭhapter Ten

"Miracles represent freedom from fear.

Ⅰ had forgotten that I'd set up the interview until the alarm woke me. My face was puffy from crying and no sleep. The head partner at Hank's office had said I would be perfect in commercial real estate. His exact words were "Anyone half as good as you are in sales could make a killing in this business. You gotta work for us." Of course, that was before Hank was rear-ended by a cigarette butt. I don't know why I hadn't canceled the appointment—greed, gluttony, materialism, and money had something to do with it. My reason was the goal and possibility of being a millionaire and retiring before I was thirty. This made me get out of my bed.

Oh, yeah, and that I wanted to get a glimpse of him. Hank. I had to see his face and to feel his pulse—or see if he had one.

Leaving the warmth of my home to go to the interview, I noticed a frozen smudge on the glass of my front door. It was Hank's fish-lip prints that he had left while waiting for me to open the door one day. Cold air can do that; it can preserve things for a long time. His lips were frozen in frost crystals outside my door—the blur brought back the memory of him. I slowly touched the glass with my index finger to wipe away the smudge but couldn't. I left it there, as if to keep a part of him in my house forever, kissing me, loving me.

Not more than an hour or so later, I was walking through the lobby after what passed for an interview. My phone rang. Pam. Her timing is sometimes impeccable.

"Well, what happened?"

I walked outside before replying. "It was a joke; there was no job. I was in and out of there in twenty minutes."

"Did you see Hank?"

"M-I-A," I said, the phone cradled to my neck as I opened the car door.

"Frat boys always stick together. Come on. Let's go out tonight. There's this great new club on Ninth."

"You go, and find one for me." I gave her back one of her own lines.

In my car, I hit the CD button, and Reggae Head came on. The Caribbean rhythm's sweet, smoky pulse urged me to forget my troubles—don't worry—but I wasn't buying it. I was too numb.

The confidence I'd felt with Hank, so like what I'd once felt as a child, was gone. It was replaced by a familiar hollow feeling of not being good enough, smart enough, graceful or thin enough, first in my father's eyes and now in Hank's.

I had told Hank I was the least-educated in my family, where multiple master's degrees and PhD's were the norm. But I didn't tell him I tried to finish college three times and then gave up. I would enroll and then when the tuition needed to be paid or I needed to choose courses, I would freeze and never attend. I started to believe I was the failure my father thought I was. I bombed my SATs twice in high school.

In grade school, I had to go to *special* reading classes. All the kids knew about those rooms. I never understood why I had to go there in the first place, and I certainly didn't feel "special," just dumb. My father did nothing to help me think otherwise.

He was an angry guy, strict and very overprotective— and that's the good stuff. My mother called it controlling but stifling was more like it. In our household, curfews were so early that I had to be home before the sun set, and that was in high school. I didn't grow up in the Middle Ages, so it was a big deal. In the summertime there was no use going out, because as soon as I got somewhere fun, I'd have to head home. The upside to my restricted and controlled childhood was that if I finished my homework and did my chores perfectly before dinner, I was allowed to play in the neighborhood. Outside, there was no one saying things like, "Why don't you stick with ballet? It could really help you. You know, if you focused more, you wouldn't trip all the time," or "Don't you think the reading classes are helping you, Ryley?" You'd think instead of putting me in ballet classes, he could have at least checked me for inner ear problems.

My best escapes were when my sister was nose-deep in one of her many literary classics. She could block out my father's rage—his breaking dishes, swearing at my mother, and slamming doors. I would creep down the steps past my father's office and head directly to the garage. My sister's bike was always locked, but I knew the combination. I'd slip it out the side door, making sure no one heard the garage door open. The journey would be a long expedition around the block, but I had no fear, only the love of being in the full moment. Her bike had the hand brakes. It was a teenager's bike—my bike was too small and still carried the scars where the training wheels once had been. I could go faster and farther on hers.

With the wind blowing in my face from pedaling as fast

as I could, I believed I was invincible. I felt as if some invisible force was keeping me company all the time, protecting me, loving me—sort of an invisible friend but bigger. I'd linger in the daydream with every push of the pedal.

Somewhere along the way, I'd left my childhood behind. My spiritual companion went the way of invisible friends, and the thrill of closing a deal dulled the edges of my father's disapproval. Who cared about a master's degree if I'd socked away my first million by age thirty? In the real world, not in my high-strung educated family, *that* is what counted. My childlike imagination dissipated because my fears increased, leaving me with an adult sense of reality and a broken heart that ached.

It didn't matter that Triangle Brokers would not hire me. I wouldn't have taken the job anyway. I had a job, and it paid my bills with a lot left over. The real problem was the fact that my office was in a luxurious building that was one of Hank's accounts. I knew I'd run into him and didn't want to.

Getting Hank's face, movements, words, and scent out of my system wasn't easy. He was everywhere and in everything. The memory of him was thick in the produce department at Wegman's Supermarket when I was picking up takeout. He was the one who taught me how to pick a good mango and look for a ripe avocado, as well as smell that perfect smell in a melon—produce was now off limits.

I kept thinking I saw him in the checkout line. All of a sudden, it seemed as if every man over six feet was Hank, until he'd turn around and it was a stranger. I could feel his breath on my skin. I missed him. I wanted him—that unshaven face, scruffy and fierce under my covers. Where was he?

Nowhere. Absolutely nowhere. How do you let go of

someone when he is so much a part of you? Your heart, your life.

Sarah once told me that the red deer bellows a nonstop love call, over and over, for several days. "It apparently is quite effective at introducing reproductive readiness." If I bellowed, "Please come back, Hank, please come back," could I keep it up for several days? Would he hear? Would it work? Or would a bunch of deer come knocking at my door?

I knew what was really driving me crazy. It was the stuff Fran had said. I thought I would never believe in reincarnation. Now, it was a possibility, an explanation of why I could not separate my mind, body, and soul from his.

Depression came on fast and hard. My heart was still and numb, like it was locked inside a dead hollow tree. My branches were ready to snap in a moment. My gloom had a low rumble that wallowed in my throat, lapped against tears that were never far from the surface. And when they broke, they flowed down my face like tiny rivers.

Not only was Hank missing in my life, but I was missing too. I felt disconnected, ungrounded, and muddled. My body floated and bobbed from work to home to bed, from bed to work and back again. Looking into a mirror with bloodshot eyes, I realized I had poured myself into something outside of myself and couldn't find my way back in.

Sarah and Pam kept calling, and I kept blowing them off. No energy to talk. No energy to speak. But Sarah was persistent—too persistent—and showed up one night when I was asleep, in bed with stockings, bra, and shirt left on from work.

"Hey, I brought you something." She was holding a box of herbal yogi tea labeled *Detox*—rich in organic cardamom seed, flower extracts, and a proprietary blend of herbs.

"Go away. I don't want to pee all night."

"No, goofball, the tea's for me. This is what's for you."

Out of a yellow-and-blue paisley-and-floral backpack, she pulled a thick dossier filled with blank parchment paper.

"This is going to make you feel so much better."

I was hoping for ice cream or chocolate, not parchment paper.

"Letter burning!" she exclaimed with too much enthusiasm.

"What?"

"This is what I want you to do: Take as many sheets as you need and write down every feeling, every thought, everything you wished you'd said to him, everything you want to say but would never say; swear, purge, just get it all out, every last word until you cannot write one more. And then you burn it!"

"Burn it?"

"Yes, and you'll see the heaviness, the immensity of what you are fearing and feeling ... melt away ... burn away. And I promise you, you'll feel so much better."

"You're kidding, right?"

"Rye, I'm serious. It works!"

"Oh, God, Toad."

"Just do it!"

Before she left, she turned to me. "Love hurts—it can even kill. For certain insects—the Australian redback spider to be precise—boy meets girl. Girl eats boy." She smiled.

I smiled back.

And she left as swiftly as she'd come.

I wrote a letter on the heavy parchment paper. Sentences filled with hurt, anger, and rage. *Hank, you liar. You said you love me. My heart hurts, it really hurts ... were you fucking her when you were with me? Were you telling her the same things you told me? I feel so heavy so sad."* My hands went numb from holding the pen too tightly as I composed letters in dark ink, a one-sided conversation.

I sank deeply into my sofa and pulled my knees toward my face. A broken voice came out from within. I wanted to swear at Hank, swear at Elizabett, and swear at God. I looked at the parchment pad and saw my words there, cold and angry, leaving tortured marks and a mess of scribbled chaos.

When finished, I took each page to the kitchen sink and lit the corners with a wooden match, watching the words melt into small flames. With each flicker, the flames dissolved the words as well as the heaviness in my heart. The burning pages left me with scorched fingertips and a light head. What do you know? Toad was onto something here.

As the days slowly moved on, the melancholy crept back into my system, making my heart wobbly, but the rhythm of my heartbeat was coming back, reminding me that I was still here; I would survive.

The late evenings were the loneliest. I'd stare out my window and watch the trees for hours. Even though the winter wind was bitter, there was something about the movement of the few leaves on the branches that gave me hope and solace. I found myself picking up the strange book again.

My grievances hide the light of the world in me. I cannot see what I have hidden. Yet I want it to be revealed to me.

I found an exercise that involved visualizing my mind surrounded by a layer of heavy, dark clouds that hid a brilliant light. The exercise instructed me to settle down in perfect stillness and be determined to go past the clouds, to reach out and touch them with my mind and brush them aside with my hand, feeling them rest on my cheeks and forehead and eyelids as I went through them. *Clouds cannot stop you. Be determined; call on the power of the universe to help you, and God will raise you from darkness into light. You cannot fail because your will is the same as God's.*

I could hear Sarah saying, "If you're willing to take a break and breathe, to pause for a moment and be still enough to look inside of you, you would see and get in touch with what is in all of us—unconditional love."

Forget it.

I couldn't get it. This crazy course suggested that the pain I was feeling was an illusion and that my desperation wasn't real. It was real to me. The book went back on the shelf. I wasn't ready to move out of my pain. I was moving through my life, alone.

Chapter Eleven

"Miracles should inspire gratitude, not awe."

With spring comes new beginnings. White and purple crocuses were popping their heads through the muddy earth in my front yard as the days became longer and warmer. After six weeks of feeling sorry for myself and wallowing in my wounded-soldier gray period, I came up for air and realized something had to change. And if something had to change, I was going to change it. No, I wasn't going to cut my hair. The alluring solution that I hit upon was finding a new job. Why not? The company that I was working for wasn't ever going to promote me—I was too valuable as a salesperson. I wanted management. Management was where the real money was.

I had to get out of Hank's building. I had run into him once when he was showing office space to a prospective client, and once was enough.

The client was checking out the space on the ground floor, and Hank was waiting in the main lobby. I was running late to an appointment and ran into him—literally.

"Hey, Ryley," he said, with eyes cast downward as I righted myself and pulled away.

"Hey" was all I said.

He grabbed my elbow as I skirted past.

He swallowed, unable to speak for a few seconds. "Hey,

how are you?" His eyes went soft. "I … I'm … how've you been?" His expression was all sympathy, apologetic, even concerned, as if to say, "I'm sorry this has been brought on you."

There it was, out in the open, and I was in no mood to get drippy, so I held in there strong, and with a great smile, said, "Fine. Life moves on." I had to give him a show, pretending what happened between us was nothing, a shake of the wrist, nothing. Even though it was everything.

He froze. His face shifted—hurt, surprise—then formed into a polite mask.

I did it. I got a rise out of him.

"See ya," I said as I dashed to the door and out to fresh air.

He said nothing, unable to move.

It was time to get out of his space, immediately. After seeing him, I searched everywhere for a new job: online, newspapers, headhunters. You name it, I tried it. I consulted a book that defined success in sales management and came up with the perfect solution and strategy.

Number one. Opportunity: bigger company, like a Fortune 100 or 500, more benefits, better medical and better 401(k), more money, and a management program.

Number two. Personal: good location, close to the house, with a possible gym and showers.

Number three. Hank factor: no more of Hank's buildings.

After driving my headhunter crazy with my pickiness, she actually found it.

The office building was what Hank would have referred to as class-A space. Deluxe everything—lobby, cafeterias (yep, more than one place to snack), gym locker room with marble sinks, windows with the views of large oak trees and grassy hills. Best of all, I would have a private cubicle with its own door. No more whispering on private calls.

My headhunter informed me there were forty-plus candidates going after the same job. I arrived at the second interview, nervous but confident. I was escorted from the large and exquisite lobby to a massive corner office that belonged to the man who was interviewing me. He headed the region and would be my boss's boss. The head cheese in the local sneeze.

As I sat in one of the chairs that faced the large cherry desk, I took in the space. Floor-to-ceiling windows on two sides that overlooked rolling hills. The room was so big, my kitchen, dining room, and part of my living room would have fit in it. I felt small in such an enormous space. Where were the red carpet and throne?

My eyes searched quickly for any clues about the man who would soon interview me. His desk was bare, with the exception of a neat and tidy stack of papers on the upper left-hand corner. This meager sign suggested he was either an anal-retentive clean freak or had nothing to do. There was an empty folder with just my name on it, strategically placed in the center of his desk, as if to say, "Here lies the commencement of the next event of the day." Who'd put it there? His secretary? Human resources? Or had he placed it there, so straight and precise, showing me that he might be rigid, inflexible, and unbendable?

I wanted to peek inside the folder but couldn't run the risk of being caught. There were no pictures of a wife or kids or dog or friend. No diplomas on the wall, no pointers whatsoever. It was almost sterile.

"Hello, Ryley," he said, as he walked into the office, scaring me half to death. He was very tall, dark, and handsome, with eyes that shot right through me—the color of the sky on a clear blue day. His hair, slightly receding, was smooth and black, with a hint of salt and pepper at the temples. Not a strand out of place, moussed to perfection. He wore a black suit that looked like it wanted to be something really expensive but wasn't. Great tie—trendy but not over the top. And then there were those suspenders that were surprisingly sexy. I wanted to snap them right on his chest.

"Hello," I returned, standing and greeting him with a firm handshake. Wow, not bad for a boss's boss.

When he spoke, he had charisma and fire, while maintaining a professional demeanor. He asked all the typical interview questions. I felt as if I were dazzling him, or maybe it was me who was being dazzled. The chemistry became clear, making me nervous, fidgety, and self-conscious, not for fear of not getting the job but because this man could make me spark. What was it about a man in a suit, a crisp white shirt, and wingtips?

It was odd. I felt like I was being unfaithful to Hank for feeling this way. But why? There was no Hank.

He outlined the enticing job. There was a personal sales support person for the position, no cold-calling, sixty percent travel, and a management trainee program required upon acceptance. It was too good to be true. I was astonished that the company actually was considering me for the job.

His eyes sparkled with intelligence. He had a whimsical way of explaining things—a lively interest that was intoxicating. But I let the chemistry subside. Office romances were a huge faux pas. No fishing off the company pier.

Interesting. There was life after Hank. This was a glimpse of it, and it filled me with confidence. By golly, I was getting over Hank.

Forty-seven people applied for the position. In my second

interview, he leaked that I was one of the top three candidates. I asked what it would take to be number one, but he never gave me a straight answer.

I must have done something right, because three days later, the company called to offer me the job.

Sarah called right after.

"I got the job!" I almost screamed.

"I'm coming over. I've got good news, too!"

When she came into the living room, I swung her around in a bear hug. We jumped around the house and bounced on my bed like a couple of two-year-olds. Sarah finally told me why she was so excited. "You are not going to believe it. I got a promotion!"

"Get out of here! How long were you going to wait until you told me?"

"Until I knew it was final.'

"And?"

"And I think I'm flipping out. They gave me a thirty-five percent bump in pay, an actual office, and a new title."

"Oh, my God, you're Dr. Jekyll!"

She threw a pillow at me. Her giggle came back, and it was as if we were teenagers again. We topped our girlfriend high with a cherry and went shopping. Shopping with my best girlfriend, and a reason to buy and having the money to do it—nothing better. We hit all the sale racks and all the favorite spots and walked away with a ton of good loot.

So my closet was updated with new suits, blazers, and skirts. The old, drab clothes were given to Goodwill. I had a new closet and a brand-new outlook. I was ready for a new beginning and to knock 'em dead at my new job.

And then it began. My first day at General Telephone— or as everyone called it, GT.

I was nervous the first week, trying to find my way around

the office, taking in new processes, getting things organized, learning new product material, and getting to know people. I observed and tried to feel out who was going to be helpful, who were the sticks-in-the-mud, who would become friends and allies, how things were run. More importantly, I had to figure out who was really in charge and who actually got things done in a pinch. The usual new-job stuff. The key was to act friendly and just watch—don't interfere, don't get in the way, don't be nosy or try to change things until I had won them all over. The only way I would do that was to bring in the largest sales the company had ever seen and to do it humbly.

I had to earn respect if I ever was going to get into management. I was up for the challenge. The good news was that the company exceeded my expectations. I had no idea a company could be so organized and have such quality people. But then again, it was early on in the job.

As the first weeks rolled by, I made my new home in my cube with a view. A small, yellow, flowering plant nestled in one of my white-and-blue oriental pots. Pictures of my family from last Thanksgiving were framed in teak inlaid wood, along with one of my favorite pictures of Toad and me at her parents' summer home in Cape Cod.

When no one was around late one night, I even put up soft-yellow country-French wallpaper. I tacked it up with a staple gun, and it made all the difference. In the center of my desk was an old desk lamp with a low-watt bulb from home. A glow emanated from the lamp and warmed my cubicle, displacing the horrible fluorescent light from above. My fellow senior sales reps made fun of my office; they suggested it belonged on the home decorating channel. I ignored them. This was the new headquarters of Look Out, Baby; Sales are Going to Fly.

After close to a month on the job, I noticed that the attractive man from my interview, Richard, was either being very friendly or eye-balling me. As magnetic and charismatic as he was, I kept my distance. It wasn't easy, but this was the time to get things done and get my footing. No more moping over Hank. I was back on the game; I was getting to the office before everyone and staying later than anyone. No one could get in the way of my success, not even Mr. Tall, Dark, and Handsome. There was a lot of work to do if I were to be the number one rep in the company.

———

It was especially late on a Friday; I was in the copy room in the back of the large office. Richard and I were the only two left in the building. I was making copies on converging voice and data networks, preparing for my appointments the following week. Richard leisurely thumbed through his mail. I thought it was strange. Normally, secretaries take care of the mail. Executives rarely enter the door of the copy room. Was something else on his mind? I tried to stay cool, professional.

"You're here late, Ryley."

"Yeah," I said, my eyes glued to the flashing lights of the copier.

"How are things going on the Syracuse accounts?" he asked. His tone was warm and sunny.

"Really well," I said, barely raising my eyes.

"It's pretty late ... have you eaten?"

"Oh, I'm heading home soon."

"If you wanna, we could grab a bite and go over the Syracuse market."

I was stuck.

Here was my boss's boss. He made it sound work-related.

If I said no, he might think I didn't want to put in the extra work or gain his insight about the job. If I wanted to get into management, dinner would be my opportunity to campaign and position myself.

In the back of my mind, something felt wrong about going to dinner with Richard, like his intentions might not be honorable. But I went anyway. If I were a guy, it would be no big deal, but I wasn't, so it was.

Chapter Twelve

"In my defenselessness my safety lies."

Once in my car, I picked up my cell phone for an emergency call to Pam.

"OK, I'm about to have dinner with my boss's boss. Fast—what do I do?"

"You gotta give me more than that." I gave her the details. "No problem. Just act cool; make it all about business. Stay the business course. Let him lead."

"What if he starts flirting?"

"Smile, but don't flirt back."

We went to a Thai restaurant and, as he'd promised, we talked about the Syracuse market and my accounts and as many aspects of my job as he could think of. When the food came, Richard grinned and said, "I love spicy food."

"I can see that."

"I'm trying to increase my capsaicin tolerance level."

"I'm sorry?"

"When spicy food hits your tongue, capsaicin receptors in your mouth's cell membranes send a rush of pain to command central. Your brain thinks it's under attack and releases a flood of endorphins to fight back."

"Really ... so you get an endorphin high, kinda like a drug response?"

"Exactly. You can get hooked on the stuff."

"Oh, I see."

He had amazingly strong but sensitive hands—his fingers were long but not too thin and had not one callus. One hand was whiter than the other, from what I found out later was his golf glove. His nose was uneventful, and he wore glasses that looked natural on his face.

His mustache gave me some pause—trendy mustaches have never been my thing, but it wasn't too bad on him.

He saw that I was relaxing, so with a straight face and the tiniest kidding tone, he said, "I really wish you'd stop staring at me all the time at work."

I blurted out a laugh. "What!"

"Your shameless flirting has got to stop—I gotta concentrate on work." His kidding continued, but he toned it down because he was testing how far he could go with it. I didn't give in; I stayed grounded in my professionalism but wasn't stiff.

There was something very odd. Don't ask me how, but he was pulling me in. His easy charm was mesmerizing. He told stories with infinite details that made me feel part of the narrative. He used his hands when he talked, and his movements were strong and tender, as if he could bend a fork with a velvet glove. It was a type of hand a hummingbird might fly into to find shelter. I wanted to fly in too. When he talked about something, it was so infectious that I suddenly wanted to do what he was talking about. He made the ordinary parts of work sound extraordinary.

And every now and then, there was a glimpse at his mysterious, dark side. His smile would vanish. Then as quickly as the smile vanished, it would return.

"Do you live with your boyfriend?" he asked.

"Well … I don't have one." I couldn't believe I told him.

"Are you sure?" he said in an exaggerated tone, as if he couldn't believe it.

"Yes, I think I'd notice one if he were hanging around."

"Why don't you have a boyfriend? Are you a serial murderer? Psychopath? Lesbian? Abused? What's wrong with you?"

I laughed.

Even though he could make me laugh, and he was fascinating, I wouldn't have to worry that this would turn into an office romance. Yes, there was chemistry, but my guess was that we would just become friends or have great rapport at work.

Outside, after dinner, he took out a cigarette and offered me one. I shook my head as the chemistry dissipated.

Later that week, I was off to Syracuse for my first business trip. Never having been on a trip paid by my employer, I was excited, to say the least. GT was not cheap. No Comfort Inns; it was Hyatt or Four Seasons all the way. The Hyatt in Syracuse was brand new, offering class, comfort, and convenience for the pampered professional. I could get used to this.

I had a small suite. To the right of the entry was an alcove that housed a large, cherry desk equipped with fax, phone, and DSL connection. I was told the entire hotel also had a wireless network, so I could use my laptop anywhere in my room. It was the little touches that impressed me: pencils, pens, staplers, Post-it notes, paper clips, tape. Who needed an office? It was all here. A sitting area was on the opposite side, with a soft and elegant sofa next to an oversized chair and ottoman. Fresh flowers were centered on the coffee table. Straight in front was a king-sized bed with striped silk duvet and endless pillows. Lying on top of the bed was a thick, white terrycloth robe that screamed, "Put me on!" And, as you might guess, on top of the largest pillows were Belgian chocolates that were to die for.

I slipped on the robe and called Sarah. "Toad, you are not going to believe where I am calling you from," I said, eating the last bite of the chocolates.

She and I caught up on the past few days. With her promotion, she had been working as hard as I had, and we hadn't been able to hang out much at all. She updated me on the new book she was reading, *How to Improve Your Life in One Breath*. It was, of course, about meditation, and she gave me the Cliffs Notes in ten minutes. I gave her my new number, and she promised to call the next day.

Then I called Pam. "Would you date anyone from work?"

"God, no."

"Why?"

"If it doesn't work out, you're stuck in the same cage as him."

"You're starting to sound like Sarah."

"It works. Why are you asking?"

"Well, there's this guy ..."

"No, Rye."

"Well, he's kind of mysterious."

"Definitely, no!"

"Yeah, maybe you're right."

Beep. Call waiting.

"Hang on, Pam. There's another call." I switched lines. "Ryley McKenna."

"Hi, Ryley. It's Richard Stemick."

God, why would the boss's boss be calling me?

"Richard, could you hold on? I have a call on the other line." I switched back to Pam "Gotta go. Business on the other line."

"No prob. Talk to you tomorrow."

I was completely caught off guard.

He explained, "Just wanted to make sure our new senior

rep was in good hands. Are you getting the support you need?"

Blah, blah, blah. He was highly professional. Just making the rounds. He made it sound strictly like company policy. But then, the conversation turned slightly personal: Had I been to Syracuse before? Had I traveled much? Did I travel growing up? Where did I grow up? How many people in my family?

Before I knew it, we were talking about everything, more than I'd intended sharing and much more than Pam would have approved of. After a long-winded conversation, I suddenly realized it was close to midnight. I'd lost track of time. Was it his maturity, his experience in the business, his success that came with being ten years older that kept me on the phone?

Even more surprising was the next day, and the next day, and the next; we spoke every night for three weeks. When he called, it stopped being about business, "So tell me … when you are fantasizing about me, what color are my chaps?"

My laugh came from deep in my gut.

He kept me on the phone, joking and spinning stories.

"How's work?" I asked.

He said it in a straight voice but was totally kidding. "Well, my boss keeps hounding me, wanting to promote me. I wish he would stop calling all the time. Sure, I could run the company, but I'm humble, and I like my job." And then later in the conversation, he said, "You know, you're the type of perfect package that could have first choice of any guy. Why aren't they lined up? It's an absolute tragedy that there isn't a guy cooking breakfast for you every morning."

His kidding turned me on. Richard had a way of making me feel like I was the only woman on the planet. His flattery was cleverly crafted. "You're beautiful and intelligent. You are head and shoulders over any woman I have ever met. I can't believe you don't have a boyfriend." What do you do when someone says that, other than just feel good? I started to feel better about myself than I had in months.

I really blushed when he said, "I gotta tell you; you're so svelte—what a body." I thought, *Who uses "svelte"*?

I fell for his charm, sinking into it like quicksand; there was no turning back. I told myself that I shouldn't worry if I wasn't completely physically attracted to him because it's what's inside that counts.

He was more than a perfect rebound guy. He was a total brain too—he knew everything. He could quote Gandhi or Socrates in a simple way that made me wonder how his mind actually worked. We had the same philosophy of life— work first, play later. Sure, some might have seen him as a workaholic, but I saw his dedication and could relate to it. Sarah would have loved him, if I just had the courage to tell her about him. He knew odd things, as she did, about endangered species and people throughout history that I didn't even know existed. I was surprised to learn that he'd never gone to college. I found out, much later, that he was addicted to public television and the History and Discovery channels.

He was creeping into my heart and nestling there. When I lost an account or a client wouldn't buy, he'd say, "Time doesn't go backward. It happened; it's no good worrying about it. Learn from it and keep moving."

I just wished he looked more like Hank. Even with my unsure feelings about Dick, the relationship grew deeper and closer. I wondered if he was my novena, my perfect man. The truth was, I wanted the novena more than I wanted myself. I couldn't wait to get back to the office after eight weeks of travel and see him again.

Chapter Thirteen

"A miracle is never lost."

I got back from my trip just in time for the monthly branch meeting. Dick would be there. I'd only been to a few branch meetings, and I was about to be late for the first time.

I sprinted there from my cubicle, convinced I was going to be late. I did not want the unmistakable quiet and all eyeballs staring at you when you walked in late. But the absolute worst part was when the person running the meeting would stop mid-sentence and give you that look of death that says, "Thanks for interrupting us. Why can't you be on time like everyone else? Remind me to kill you after the meeting."

I slowly opened the heavy mahogany door and to my great surprise, people were milling around the room, grabbing the catered food on the side credenza, and chatting noisily. They hadn't started. I snagged a bottled water and a fancy, pre-made, grilled-chicken salad in a plastic container and made my way to one of the remaining leather conference chairs.

The meeting was in GT's largest conference room, one that was ideal for presentations. There was a huge whiteboard and state-of-the-art digital multimedia equipment that ran along both sides of the room. Two people could present at once, even though that never happened. The conference table was a dark, glossy wood, longer than two end-to-end station wagons. The best part of the room was the chairs— the womb chairs, made of the softest of leathers; they reclined. I could rock myself to sleep in those chairs; in most of the branch meetings, I wouldn't even have to rock.

The topic for the day's meeting: Next Generation Software Release for our large-scale enhanced platforms and integration to high-performance enterprise network products. It was research and development's meeting, but the regional manager was co-chairing, so Dick would present. The intention of the meeting was to update sales and marketing on the latest and greatest products that were on the way. And to find betas (test pilots) before the actual launch so bugs could be ironed out of a new product. No smart salesperson would recommend one of their customers for a beta—offering them up as a sacrificial guinea pig to the technological wolves. Who wanted to piss off a client or worse, lose one?

It was a techno-weenie meeting, presented by the company nerds. And, of course, they would get nervous because they were presenting in front of all the hotshots in the company, so there was guaranteed super-techno-weenie talk, their language of choice. The acronyms would be flying at a rate of a billion megahertz per second. A sure snoresville meeting.

It was the perfect opportunity to sneak my hands under the table and catch up on e-mails on my CrackBerry, as Sarah called it.

Everyone settled in; some were still eating their lunches while others fidgeted in their seats. In walked Dick. I rarely saw him at work because I was either traveling or in a different part of the building. Our relationship was almost entirely on the phone at this stage. This was my chance to watch him in action.

He was dressed in typical business attire: a white oxford shirt and a navy suit. His shoes were the classic deep-brown oxfords, with laces tied in such perfect bows that I wondered if they were slip-ons. No tie; he was trying to be casual for the technical staff. He had helmet head: his hair was perfectly coiffed and moussed. I wanted to chuckle. Was that hair on purpose? He looked goofy but cute. I remembered his line from our first dinner: "I really wish you'd stop staring at me all the time." I wanted to laugh.

One thing was for sure: The guy had charisma. To suggest that he had the ability to work a crowd, captivating us with even the most boring material, would be like saying that Mother Teresa was just a nice gal. He was hot, and I wanted to nail him right there on the conference table. Watching Dick work his magic, with his 3-D graphs that rotated and pivoted as he spoke about how our new technology product suite worked, made me want to do things I'd never done before.

Even more exciting was the fact that I knew him so well because of our daily calls. The sheer fact that I knew things about this man that no one else knew—or even had a clue about—was arousing. I could hide, blend into the audience, and fantasize about the wildest and craziest things, and not a soul could get into my head to check out my internal movie screen. There was an illicit element—a tantalizing blend of power and scenery that heightened my attraction to this man.

Finally, after I'd been home after weeks of travel, it was one-on-one time with Toad. We were snuggled into wicker chairs, artfully arranged on her screened-in back porch. As we sipped freshly brewed iced tea with mint leaves, she filled me in on everything that was going on with her; I filled her in on Dick.

I knew that when Sarah asked a lot of questions, she was secretly judging him. "So what's he like, exactly, other than intellectual and funny? Where are his roots?"

"He's from a small town in Michigan and has a sister and brother. He's in the middle. He comes from a divorced family. I think the father cheated on their mom. He tells me his mom's a saint, and I believe him." I was leaving stuff out— like the conversation I had with him on the phone about the divorce. He had said, "It really hit me hard. I was only twenty-three years old. I was forced to live with my mom in a trailer." When he said that, I wanted to laugh at the absurdity of it, but he was serious. Did he actually think living at home at twenty-three wasn't a choice? But then it got worse: "My sister and I were separated for the first time. When you go through stuff like that, it shows you the real person you are ... I feel like I'm stronger for that."

Toad was still drilling me with questions: "Where did he go to college?"

"He didn't."

"And he's an intellectual? How?"

"He reads a lot and is one of those types that, if he'd had a chance, would have graduated magna cum laude at the best university."

"Then why didn't he?"

"He got his girlfriend pregnant when he was still living at home and being a good Catholic boy. He married her."

"What happened to her?"

"They had three kids, but it didn't work out."

"Why?"

"Because they were too young. I don't know ... 'cause they wanted different things."

"What did he want?"

"To get out of a dead-end job in Michigan and start over."

"And did he?"

"Yeah. He moved to Chicago, worked in the mailroom of GT, and worked his way up. Married again, but it didn't work out. Got promoted and moved to New York."

"He's been married twice?"

"He started young."

"Well, how old is he?"

"He's thirty-four."

"He's ten years older than you?"

"Yeah."

I wished she would just stop it. She made him sound so bad, and he wasn't—he was good. I had to try to plead my case.

"Toad, you don't get it. It's his ability to make something from nothing that is so remarkable. He's the most intellectually astute and business-savvy guy I know, and he did it all on his own."

"Don't you think his wives might have helped?"

"No."

"Why is it that he's so young and has been married twice, and the marriages didn't work out?"

"I don't think he plays the field. I think he's a one-woman type."

"There is one thing truly unusual in nature—monogamy. The only mammal I can think of that is monogamous is the chinstrap penguin. Staying faithful is their shrewdest reproductive strategy of all."

There was something inexplicably wounded in her eyes as she gave me her analogy of life, something wary and frightened in the way she met the world. Oh, Toad, behind her scientific talk she was so innocent and vulnerable. I wanted to tell her not to be scared. Men could be good.

"Sometimes you've just got to take a chance. Open your

heart and breathe in for a moment. Isn't that what you are always teaching me?"

She finally took a break from the line of questioning. A short one. "What did he do before GT?"

"Sales. I think he was a car salesman."

"Hmm. What type?'

"Used."

"Oh, God, Rye!" she exclaimed, as if she'd just found the missing link.

"Shouldn't you be finding the cure for shut up?" I was so pissed.

She stopped. She let it go. I knew she was projecting the stuff she feared most in her heart—fear of commitment, fear of loving a man. But the truth is she was also bringing up all the things I had wondered about, but I didn't want to go there.

I didn't have the guts to tell her the weird stuff, like he was fanatical about not being seen in public. And I mean fanatical. I understood that we shouldn't be seen together because he was my boss and we worked together, but I mean, come on. We rarely went out and when we did, it was to the grungiest dives in the farthest reaches of America. The whole thing was too rehearsed; we drove in separate cars, went at separate times, and had to act like we were bumping into each other. We had a speech, just in case we did bump into someone, which never ever happened. I understood corporate politics, but he was way beyond extreme. Sure, he'd joke, like saying, "You know I don't like going where the paparazzi can find me." But he really wasn't joking.

I told myself that relationships weren't fairy tales. Perfect relationships just didn't exist. My relationship with Dick was something I had to work at to make it right, to make it fit. I wondered if I was making Dick into something that he wasn't. I ignored the signs that screamed "Danger! Danger! Clear the area! Bad relationship ahead!"

Chapter Fourteen

"Let all things be exactly the way that they are."

Hank called.

On a hot summer day, out of the blue, right when I was starting to let the memory of him fade, he called. It's not like I hadn't run into him; I had. He wanted to do lunch or drinks and insisted that we remain friends, but I think he might have wanted more, and I think I did, too. I couldn't do it. I had let him down gently the handful of times that we'd run into each other. Like the last time, when he called me at home.

"I'm seeing someone," I said, wiping my brow, which was damp from the humid August heat.

"Who?" he asked, as if I had just shot him with a silver bullet through the heart.

"Oh, you don't know him," I said, turning on the air conditioner.

"I might."

"Richard Stemick."

"The car salesman?"

"No, he works for GT," I said, pulling and pumping the T-shirt from my armpits to get some air in.

"Yeah, that's now! He came to me for space. The guy's a snake."

"Are you jealous?" I turned up the air conditioner, hoping the cool air would speed up.

"You're too good for him, Ryley. Be careful."

There it was again, his brilliance. I'm too good for Dick but not good enough for Hank. I had to go and heave.

"Nice chatting."

"How about lunch?"

"Sorry, I'm jammed."

Maybe Sarah was right. Life without men—a novel idea. Might not be a bad thing. No matter how mismatched my relationship was, no matter how unstable the feelings I had for Dick, I was loyal. A foreign concept to Hank. And as much as I missed Hank, I stayed away. I thought I was doing OK. I really did.

Then it happened—the day light stopped shining on the planet.

Out of the blue, Hank called me at home to announce the big news. I couldn't remember when we'd spoken last. It seemed like an eon since he'd dumped me.

I picked up the phone, and there he was, saying, "Hi."

"Hi"—it was all he said. It was all he ever said. He always assumed that I knew who it was. Well, of course I knew; I just hated the fact he never announced himself.

"Hi?" I asked, pretending I didn't know.

"It's me."

I still didn't say anything.

"Hank."

"Oh, hi. What's up?" The epitome of aloof.

"How are you doing?"

"Fine."

Silence.

"Well. There's something I wanted to tell you." In my

heart, I was hoping he would tell me that he'd left Elizabett and wanted to start over and that he had never stopped loving me. That he wanted a second chance. That I was the only one he ever loved.

"Ryley, I wanted you to hear it first from me."

Blood drained from my face. This didn't sound good.

"I'm getting married," he said cautiously.

Silence. Stunned. Speechless.

He continued, "They were going to deport Elizabett. The immigration office came pounding on the door and literally hauled her off. I felt responsible." His speech became quicker and quicker. "Well, she's a friend, and I couldn't bear to see her that way. She doesn't even have a green card ..."

What the hell was he talking about? She was an illegal alien? Alien, yes, but illegal too? It was too weird; I was wondering why he was making this up.

"What are you talking about? I thought she was from Illinois," I said. The sun was so bright, it blinded me when I looked out the window.

"I never told you—she's Danish and only had a temporary visa."

"I thought you said you didn't love her," I said, barely in a whisper.

His speech was flat. "Well, she's a friend, and we've known each other so long. We've been through a lot ... and ... I feel responsible ..."

My mind drifted; I was barely hearing the words. I couldn't feel anymore. I had thought that I was over him—but apparently not.

His words came back into focus. "It's like a shotgun wedding. I have to do what's right."

"So you really do love her," I mouthed, almost to myself.

"I have to do what's right," he said again.

"Well, I wish you both the best of luck," I said as sincerely as I possibly could, my voice stranger and louder than I'd meant it to be. "I'm sure you're doing the respectable thing."

"I'm trapped. I have no other choice. I really care about you. I really do."

Where was the commode? I wanted to go in head first.

"Take care, Hank. Best wishes to Elizabett."

Click.

My heart was scorched, mutilated, maimed. Give me a break; couldn't he have come up with something better? He should have just told me the truth, whatever that was.

The psychic was right about something anyway: Eight months later Dick got a transfer to California, and I tagged along. He'd promised we'd become engaged. I had nothing left to lose.

Chapter Fifteen

"Only my condemnation injures me."

I hated LA when I first arrived. The smog. The traffic. Dick.

To start off with, there were endless cars and freeways that should have been called parking lots. All the houses looked like Taco Bells—stucco with tile roofs. No Cape Cods or colonials, no hills or thick, green woods of maple or pine; just pink stucco tract houses, a million all in a row—multi-clump developments. Everything was sun-baked—dry or dead. It was hard to believe it was fall. Every day was the same.

I couldn't get my bearings, not because I didn't know where anything was, but because I had no sense of the seasons. It was like I was a fly trapped between two windows. I couldn't get out or come in—a constant state of seventy degrees with no variation. The locals said the seasons were subtle. No one had the guts to tell them that the seasons were non-existent. So they judged the season by the color of the natural grass that didn't grow in their manicured lawns. Brown was summer; green was late winter. I was stumped and wanted autumn leaves and snow and crisp sweater weather.

There were endless theme parks, dried-up reservoirs, mountains, and hillsides. There was no master plan to the development, just one continuous row of cement. Everything was excessively new and overdeveloped.

Everything had to be made beautiful instead of just being. Even the people. The land of the beautiful people: store-bought hair, bodies, boobs, and dispositions, too. And no one swore. Anything four-lettered that wasn't darn or gosh received a look of surprise and disappointment that was enough to send you back home, where you belonged.

Dick had been out-of-body excited about California. His career in New York was distressing, to say the least. The office staff complained to senior management that it didn't like or trust him. My cubicle was within earshot of all the hubbub, so I heard it all.

Almost all of his direct reports and most of the sales reps rallied against him, bashing him for the poor results of the region. I didn't get it. He was the best when it came to business strategy, leadership, and motivation. What was their problem? They blamed him for poor R and D, technical support, and even the economy, stating, "You can't sell if the product doesn't perform or if the customer is feeling pinched." Dick wasn't the problem; he was their scapegoat.

California was his way out. The economy was booming there, and he needed a fresh start. Dick convinced me that the problems in our relationship were due to the sneaking and tiptoeing around. "We wouldn't have to duck and hide. It's our chance for a normal relationship."

And part of his plan for a fresh start in California included my leaving the company and getting my own fresh start, somewhere other than GT.

I wasn't buying it.

He referred to his own career as being in the "shit basket." Mine, on the other hand, wasn't. I really loved my job. I was up for a promotion, made more money than ever before, and liked my customers. And despite what people said about Dick, they were nice to me. For me to quit my job and move to a place with no friends or family, a place that didn't have seasons, wasn't going to happen. I wasn't going to look for a job. I wanted to keep the one I had.

He gave me a firm commitment—kind of.

The conversation started in his place in Rochester, after the announcement that his transfer was solid. We stood in the center of the kitchen; he was leaning against the custom granite island. Barely above his head hung copper pots and pans that looked like a mismatched halo. They were meticulously organized on their rack, strategically placed by size and shape, larger on one side, smaller on the other. There was the next layer of placement: copper versus aluminum and steel. The handles of every pot were exactly spaced in precise parallel lines; a ruler could be taken to confirm their placement. Dick was one of those "cleanliness is next to godliness" types. But he didn't believe in God so I wondered, what was the point?

"If you're asking about my feelings for ya, Ryley, someday I see us married."

That didn't grab me.

"I'm the luckiest motherfucker in the whole world to have someone like you," he said through nicotine-stained teeth.

That definitely didn't grab me.

"Go get a ring, if that's what you want."

He placed his large, beautiful hands on my shoulders. His fingers delicately found their way to my face, where they etched my chin and cheekbones. He softly leaned against me; the refrigerator felt cold on my elbows.

"Come on, California will be fun. I want you to come with me."

He tried to look into my eyes, but I turned away and gently moved from under the weight of his hands. I was quiet and not ready to answer. He really didn't get it.

He really didn't get me.

In that moment, I felt like no one could understand how I felt, no one could get me. For some odd reason, in Dick's perfect kitchen I began to think about raspberries. Maybe because it's the way no one understands raspberries the way that I do. The way the tiny fruit rests on its thorny vines and clings so delicately. No one understands the hunt like I do; picking the most perfectly shaped and ripest berries, so full of fruit and nectar that if you're not careful, their blood will stain you, leaving their mark that lasts for at least a day.

I used to pick raspberries as a child on an island in Maine. It was my task to fill a yellow and red bowl to the rim with only the juiciest and plumpest berries. My reward would be the first piece of Mrs. Hoogen's raspberry pie. This masterpiece was between a torte and pie, gourmet and delicious. Nothing since had come close to that pie—the crust melting in my mouth and the berries in their sweet syrupy filling. It was beyond perfection.

No one understands raspberries the way I do, including Dick. He was not the one who persuaded me to go to California.

The thing that brought me to California wasn't necessarily my prospects with Dick but the prospects in my career. On an overcast and dreary morning in New York, I picked up the *Los Angeles Times* and was blown away by the opportunities. I had no idea California was so innovative and rich in strong technological companies. As fate would have it, I found more than ten remarkable companies I would have been proud to work for.

Phone calls were made, résumés sent, and when it came

time, I went out for interviews as Dick went house hunting.
There was no need for a headhunter. For some unknown
reason, Californians like New Yorkers, probably because we
know how to be workaholics. After narrowing my offers
down to three, I took the job that was head and shoulders
above my job at GT. California was a way to get into middle
management and cruise up the corporate ladder. The place
under the sun was definitely my ticket to up and out.

As much as I hated California, I did love my office. My
first *real* office, a room with two windows that was larger
than a closet and that could house more than a desk. That
first office was a coming-home party to myself. It was the
space where I could pour my heart into something and get
results greater than I could imagine—my sanctuary. I could
close my door and make a personal call; no one could hear
my conversations, even with an ear to the wall. The walls
were solid. I could look out one of my windows while on a
conference call and be somewhere else in my mind, or I
could put a call on speakerphone and walk around in the
space.

I left with Dick because I also felt like I was getting old.
It had been going on a year since I first got together with
Dick, and I would be closing in on the deadline to make a
million before I knew it. I was getting close to thirty, and
that was over the hill. I knew that someday I wanted to get
married and have kids, and it seemed easier to hang on to
what I had than to find someone new.

Before leaving New York, I picked out and bought my
own engagement ring. Dick didn't want me to wear it until
we reached California, even though the secret was out:
Everyone knew he was leaving and that I was, too.

"Baby, what do you want with a silly piece of jewelry?
It's crazy. Think of what you could do with that money," he

said with his arms around me, making me feel confused, comforted, and unworthy, all at the same time, for wanting a ring. He didn't get that a ring was my Cinderella fantasy.

I felt selfish for wanting a piece of jewelry that linked my heart to his and stupid for paying for it. "Don't worry, baby, I'll pay you back. If it's what you have to have, well, then …" He wouldn't talk about the ring, or our relationship, or commitment, or marriage. I didn't press it because I wondered about it myself. It seemed easier to stay in the relationship, because I really didn't know how things would turn out once we were in California. Maybe things would change.

Sarah was unnervingly neutral about the move. Don't get me wrong—she was upset that I was leaving her and leaving Rochester. Pam was too. But for some unknown reason, she was letting me choose my destiny on my own, without her help, without her criticism, without her input. She never came out and tried to force me to stay, but what she did say was, "If you let go of fear, you'll feel complete. When you let go of fear, what's left is love."

"Do you smoke the stuff you experiment with?" I responded.

"Remember, if you get stuck, pick up *A Course in Miracles*. Just leave it out where you can reach it—it's a process. You'll find what you need there."

"Oh, God, that book again?"

I knew she didn't like Dick, but she wouldn't say it, and it was just as well she didn't, because she didn't see his good side, his gentle side, the side that I loved.

She didn't see him on Sunday mornings, when the bedroom door would ease open as he brought a breakfast tray of gourmet delights. She didn't see the way he rubbed my feet with his large, strong hands; his soothing touch enveloping me like a warm washcloth, leaving me calm and content. He could make me feel small and safe.

But Sarah knew me and knew I was searching. My relationship with Dick reminded me of eating Pepperidge Farm goldfish crackers, the cheddar cheese ones. The first couple crackers taste so good, but after about ten, they lose that original flavor. You end up eating the whole bag because you're looking for that first taste. Dick made me feel great in the beginning, and I was still looking for that goodness.

Chapter Fifteen

"I choose the joy of God instead of pain."

Getting into the rhythm of my new job was easy; everything else took its time.

The routine of my day-to-day started to carve a pattern in my life. There was a slower pace in the flow of business in California. My typical ninety-hour week was not expected. There was a floating, radical idea of working less, slowing down, and stopping the multi-tasking. The job gave me permission to listen to my heart.

We'd been living outside of Los Angeles for more than a month. I was getting used to the lay of the land, in that I spent the majority of my days in the car, trying to get to appointments on time. A client might have been only miles away but was an hour away by car. That was a perfect time to eat, so I did.

In that first month, the engagement ring was in New York, being set. It made its way cross-country in the mail to Dick's new office. I had a feeling it had arrived, because he made me come home early for the first time ever, and he acted strangely. I played dumb when I saw the return address on the package. He was about to toss the wrapped box to me but stopped when he saw the disappointment on my face.

Instead, we got in his car and drove aimlessly because neither of us really knew the neighborhood. We were looking for a view—the sunset, maybe? We ended up in a small, run-down park, not far from home but west of it and definitely not in a good area. We drove up to an overlook—graffiti was everywhere, shards of broken glass from beer bottles, wilted condoms, low-riders. And suspicious-looking activity was going on around the cinderblock public restroom on one side of the parking lot. We were about to get out of the car but thought better of it and stayed inside.

I don't know what made Dick get out of the car, but he did. He lured me into the recreational area, and just as I was going to suggest another place, I saw him kneel. *Oh, God, not here,* I thought as he knelt under a tree, still wearing his suit from work. The naked tree had few leaves and badly peeling bark. Patches of sunlight shone on his face as his knee came crashing down on a small, speckled, brown mushroom. I knew how it felt.

"Get over here, Ryley. I have something for you. You know why I'm here. Would you marry someone like me?"

He jammed the ring on my finger.

Why didn't I say no? Stupidity. There were no violins, just boom boxes playing from crowded benches and radios blaring from Ford pickups. No sunset, no romance; just trash, beer, and the smell of pee. That wasn't the worst of it. He took me out afterward for a drink, to celebrate. Our waitress brought our champagne, and after she left, he asked, "God, wasn't she hot? I think she was checking me out." It wasn't the first time we were at a bar together and he was checking out his audience or asking me, "Don't you think it's strange the way that girl is looking at me?"

I wanted to go home to New York. Home, where it felt warm and safe, and people loved me and knew how to comfort me when my heart beat, slowed down, and ached. No one was here to help me make sense of that swirl of confusion and disappointment, the space between what one should feel and what one does feel, between the well-rehearsed fantasy and the reality.

Then, I looked at his face and saw it—saw that in his own way, he was trying. His crooked smile reminded me that there was something good deep inside him—good at heart. We were just so new to California; we just didn't know our way around, that's all. He was trying to make his life work, like all of us. He wasn't bad; he had just become hard. I did understand him and in that understanding, I was willing to hold on.

I couldn't make sense of it all, not even after calling Sarah, weeks later, to tell her the news.

"Wow," she said in a low whisper.

"What do you mean?"

"You happy?"

I didn't answer at first and then managed an unconvincing, "Yeah."

"So did you find a house yet?"

"Well ... actually, Dick found the house."

"What's it like?"

It was a brand-new typical California home, with dirt for a yard and no interior finishing. It was a shell of a home, where the owners got to choose the finishing, like countertops, cabinets, flooring, plumbing fixtures, and added upgrades.

"Fun. So what have you picked out?"

"Well, actually, Dick's doing that. I don't mind. He has such good taste."

"But you love to do all that stuff. Decorating's your thing."

"I'm just so busy at work. It's fine."

Silence.

Sarah continued, "So when do you close?"

I didn't exactly know, and I didn't want her to know that I didn't know. "So what's going on with you? How's work? Yoga? Taking any new classes?"

She let it go, but it was still at the forefront of my mind. I remembered clearly when we were supposed to go to the escrow office to close on the house together. I had pulled out my savings and the few investments that I had. When it was a day away, I had asked, "How's it going with the close?"

"Fine." He looked away.

"Is everything OK with the loan?" He had my share of the down payment, but I had not filled out any forms. I asked slowly, trying to look at his eyes. "Honey, when is the close date?"

His voice became angry. "Look, Ryley, I'm taking care of it. OK?" I didn't push it. I stopped asking if there was anything I could do to help with the process. He explained evasively that everything was getting pushed out.

He told me, weeks later, that he had gone to close escrow on the house himself. He "finished the paperwork for us," he said. He explained that he went alone because he didn't think my name was needed on the title. "Ryley, I'm putting the majority of the money down, so why should your name be on the title? We'll be married anyway." What he really wanted to say was, "I don't want your name on the title, because it's *my* house. My money is my money, and now your money is mine."

I gave in. It wasn't about the money; it was about love and trust, and there wasn't any. Deep inside, I was frozen, my insides hardening and numb. I don't know what possessed me to stay. I suppose it was the obvious—feeling trapped, all my money tied up in his house. How could I take off? We split everything—mortgage, living expenses—except for the furniture and landscaping, which I paid for.

On the other hand, the house was gorgeous. It had to be; we were pulling in the big bucks. We dumped everything into that house, and it showed. It was a treat coming home. The three-tiered fountain outside the front door was Italian and trickled away the stress of a long day at the office.

If it didn't, the Jacuzzi flowing by waterfall into the kidney-shaped pool in the lush backyard would do the trick. I tried to look forward to sitting under the stars with bubbles tickling my chin and soothing my sore muscles. I tried to see my life as a new beginning, tried to make a home for myself. And even though the house could have appeared on the cover of the best home magazines, it was strange; the plants were always dying inside. They would lose shape and weight, then gasp for air and turn brown. I knew the feeling.

Chapter Sixteen

"Miracles make minds one in God."

At work, I could let my thoughts roam free. Dick couldn't touch my mind there. It was the place where I could daydream about Hank. As usual I was stuck in traffic, trying to gulp down lunch between lane changes. There are lots of lanes in California, so there's lots of time to eat lunch on the freeway. I spent so much time in the car, it became my own personal restaurant. I had every food group available at an arm's reach. My daydreaming became reality when I got a phone call from Hank while stuck in traffic.

"Why didn't you tell me you were moving?"

There it was again. Not even a hello, or hi, it's Hank. He assumed I'd recognize his voice. I played dumb, even though my face flushed.

"Who is this?" I said, swallowing a bite of a protein bar.

"It's me. Why didn't you at least say good-bye?"

"Me, whoth?" I asked, as a chunk of protein hit the windshield.

"Oh, c'mon, Ryley, it's Hank. You could have at least said good-bye. You have no idea what it took to get this number!"

"So, how are you, Hank?" I said, tossing the wrapper in the backseat.

"Can I see you?"

"What?"

"I'm skiing in Colorado with a bunch of buddies. Can you meet me?"

"What do you mean?"

"Skiing. Colorado. Meet me."

"When?"

"Next week."

I laughed.

"Come on, you know you can do it."

"No, I don't know." I wondered if I could still fit into my ski bibs with all the extra freeway eating.

"We're going to Vail. Clear your schedule and call me back. Same number."

"Wait a minute. Aren't you still married?"

"How many times do I have to tell you? Nothing's there! It was a shotgun wedding without the kid! I'll see you next week."

Then divorce her, I wanted to say

He just assumed that I still had the number. Well, of course I had it, but still, I hated the fact he still thought I was holding on to him—which I was, but I still hated the fact that he knew.

I wanted to go so badly, even though I was getting fatter than ever. I daydreamed about seeing him but ended up calling his work number at midnight, his time, so I could leave a message telling him I wasn't coming. I tried to push him out of my mind and get back to reality in California.

But then an e-mail came—he sent me a coupon to buy a dozen songs on iTunes. I liked the gift; I just wished there were an album on which I could have double-clicked on more than a few songs. I ended up picking from Futureheads and the Farm, with the majority plucked from the Specials' first album—now there was album that was double-click-worthy on every track. A classic, with its Caribbean ska sounds—reggae with the fusion of punk rock.

Hank's e-mails and calls were enough to keep me hanging on, but they were scattered and not frequent enough for me to trust that he really thought of me as much as I was thinking of him.

———

Time crept by and I became established in my new job and new way of life. Besides loving having my own office, I loved the freedom of being a manager and trying things I wished my managers would have done for me.

My favorite part was going on calls and closing deals with the reps. For me, the hunt and the kill were the best part of sales. The hunt—finding a good customer—and the kill—closing the business. Not the in-your-face hunt and kill, but the strategic, tactical kill, like knowing the competition better than the competition knows itself, knowing every strength and weakness of the solution for the customer, and picking only the perfect customer.

I supported my reps better than they supported themselves. I figured out where the company made most of its money and the highest margin products that could bring the reps the largest commissions and largest paychecks. I showed them how to close the best sales and when they couldn't, I closed for them. We worked well as a team and after digging, we found the vertical markets with the maximum-margin potential customers. It was a numbers game, but then it always is. Throw the spaghetti on the wall and see what sticks.

It was more than just helping the reps; I was helping myself: Their success was mine. I watched and studied the most successful managers in and out of the company. I tried to find the ingredients of management success through trial and error. I found strands of spaghetti that stuck and was relentless keeping the momentum going. Work was going well.

Then there was Dick.

And my burning question: "How do you get out when you feel so dug in?" It was more than his nicotine teeth and paunch belly that were turning me off. It was his temper. We were both getting fat, and he had a lot to say about my weight, monitoring whatever I ate. It was easy to pack on the pounds when I was in the car all the time. He had the same type of controlling nature as my father, but this wasn't about finishing my master's or sticking with ballet. This was an every-meal event with Dick. I tried to let it go, but I couldn't. And the more he criticized, the more I wanted to eat.

It was a sun-drenched Saturday in LA. I had just finished working out. My T-shirt was wet at the armpits and damp in the center of my back. I took the scenic way home, and the ocean breeze brought me life through the window. I closed my eyes at a stop sign to hear blood pulsing through my veins with each crashing wave. The sunny weather lent itself to cheery personalities, people so nice they would let you in on the freeway when it wasn't even your right-of-way.

It was a day when I didn't have to fight the urge to pick up my BlackBerry or cell whenever I was at a traffic light. I was enjoying the day without distractions.

But that changed when I got home and locked my keys in the car. I had parked right next to Dick's spanking-new company car—a black Mercury, his pride and joy. I was taking in a bag of groceries. Dick was watching football on his twenty-five-foot wide television screen, beer in one hand, cigarette in the other. As I went back to the garage to retrieve my gym bag, I realized my only set of keys was in the ignition, and the doors were locked. As much as I prodded, the doors would not open.

So I crept back inside, waited for a commercial, and reluctantly asked Dick for help.

"You did what?" he groaned as he fiercely put out his cigarette.

"It's OK. I'll just call a locksmith," I offered, heading for the phone in the kitchen.

"Oh, no, you're not! Motherfucker!" he scoffed. His teeth were clenched so tightly I thought he'd chip a tooth. "You're not embarrassing me in front of the neighbors!"

I wanted to laugh. *You're kidding, right?* The neighbors who we didn't even know and were nowhere to be seen. He felt it was no one's business what happened in our house and didn't want to expose my "idiotic behavior" to anyone.

I went back out to the garage to work on the problem in the old-fashioned way, but before I knew it, he'd snatched the coat hanger I was using to unlatch the door and shoved me too hard out of his way. I'd seen him angry but not like this. He grabbed the metal wire so forcefully out of my hand, I thought he was going to start stabbing me with it. His motions were violent and brutal as he tried to open the door. The sharp metal point on the hanger started to grate on the outside of my blue Audi, leaving scars of missing paint on the exterior. I attempted to reach out gently, to make the situation easier, but he spun around, enraged. I was scared. I thought he was about to do something he had never done before. His jaw taut, he spat, "Look at what you've done. You're so stupid!"

If I had said one more thing, he would have slapped me across the face or maybe smacked me hard. If I had inched one step closer, he would have knocked me so hard, I wouldn't have been able to breath. The sting of his strike would have been fierce. Or even if I had moved the wrong way, a way that he didn't like, he could have smashed one side of my face with a fist, hard enough to blow out a tooth. I could see it in his eyes and hear it in his voice. I knew that scary monster that takes over when someone is angry.

I had seen it before.

I backed away slowly and quietly, watching him as if I were floating outside my body. It was clear that leaving my keys in the car was no big deal, and that his violent rage was about something within him and not me. He was like a rabid dog, spinning into a storm for no reason at all.

It was a rage I had seen before from my father when I was a small child. He slapped my mother and pushed her out of the house into a thick, rainy night. It was a night of yelling. He yelled a lot. He screamed at her the most, and then at my brother and then at my sister and me. My mother took me from my bed in the middle of the night.

"Come on, honey, we're going camping."

"What?" I said, groggy.

I was awake. No one could sleep with his thunderous voice. In my mother's hand was my favorite John-John doll, and my security blanket was draped over her shoulder. She peeled away the blanket, exposing me to the chilly night air. We timidly made our way downstairs through the garage and into the car. She rolled the car down the driveway in neutral. It was pouring outside, and I was frightened and cold. Why would we go camping in the middle of the night?

As soon as my mother turned on the wipers, they frayed, and an unbearable screeching came from the metal tip of the left blade searing its way into the glass. We drove around for hours, going nowhere, with that metal blade clawing, scraping, and whining. At one point, we pulled off the road to cover the wiper blade with my white tube sock, hoping it would stop the unbearable screech.

But the blade pierced through the cotton sock and started again with its grating noise. We ended up sleeping in a parking lot that night and went home early the next day.

It was at that moment, with the scraping noise of paint being stripped from the exterior of my car, after a year of living in nothingness and silent tears, that I knew what Dick was all about, and I wanted no part of it. Some people are wounded as children and vow never to hurt anyone, ever. Others inflict that pain over and over on themselves or others. He would never be able to move beyond his pain. That's not what I wanted. I was stuck three thousand miles away from help.

I crept into the house and made my way upstairs to the spare room and locked the door. Then I picked up the phone.

I heard Sarah's familiar hello. I was crying so hard that I couldn't talk. I wished I could stop for one second so I could tell her what was going on.

"Are you OK?" she asked.

The sobs were so loud and deep that there was no room for words to come out.

"What's wrong?"

Still, not a single word.

"Ryley, breathe."

Bigger sobs and bottomless groans. I felt her love through the phone and I wanted her there so badly. Her voice held me, making speaking even harder.

"Slow. One big slow breath."

So I did.

"Another and longer."

I did again. "He's a monster. I can't do this. I want to come home."

"OK. Get on a plane."

"Sarah! You don't understand."

"Help me."

"I can't just leave. I have a job and all my savings are wrapped up in this house … and I'm engaged."

"Funny how that's last," she said in almost a whisper, but I heard her.

"Stop—I need you."

"I'm sorry. You're right. Tell me everything and don't miss a single heartbeat. I'm here."

So I did. I described every detail of the day and then went back to when we arrived in California, and I told her all the bad stuff I hadn't admitted. In that time, Dick left the house, making it easy for me to relax and talk. She listened, really listened, with sympathy and empathy that made me exhausted and wanting to go to sleep. But something made me go on. "I think he's having an affair."

"Why?"

"Because we went over to dinner to some friends of his. This couple … she works for GT in another branch, and he was flirting so badly with her. God, I couldn't stand how they looked at each other, and she's so damn skinny! You could tell he just wanted to fuck her right there on the table, food and all. He's so mean and awful, I can't stand it! I hate him! Go on, say it: 'I told you so.' I should have never come out here. Why did I put myself in this mess, right"

"Oh, Ryley … no."

"Why?"

"Because you had to do it."

"What do you mean?"

"You have to live your life. I can't change what you do in it. Only you can."

"But how do I do that?"

"Forgive yourself, let go of him, and move on. Ryley … look at *A Course in Miracles* again. It's there. It will help you. You can help you."

"Sarah!"

"I'm serious. When we're off the phone, you'll need something that will help you with the day-to-day. Now just listen: I know you can't stand all my yoga and meditating and all the self-help and spiritual books, but the truth is, it works. You know what I've been through. You know what I have had to deal with. The only way I have been able to go on and move through my life without being torn in half was to learn how to forgive—forgive my parents and myself—but the biggest part was learning how to work on really liking and actually loving myself. I know that sounds weird, but it's true. I thought that wasn't possible, but then I get glimpses that I am going to be OK, and love radiates inside and outside of me … as if God is watching over me and protecting me for the first time, and that gives me the courage to go on. But it's a process, and it takes time, so start now, because you'll need all the strength you can get to leave him. But more importantly, you need to learn to love who you are so that you can go forward."

She paused for a moment, and then, her voice calm, she asked the question I'd been asking myself: "Why Richard?"

"I don't know. I feel like I got sucked into this mess, even though I knew better, and couldn't find my way out. I didn't know how to get over Hank. I thought Richard could heal me of Hank."

"Yeah, I know … but I'm the wrong one to talk to about men. I can't explain why we make the choices we do or how long it takes to correct them. But I know you, and I know you will do it when it's right for you. Rye ..."

"Yeah?"

"I do think Dick is like your dad."

"I know, I know."

"You don't have to marry your dad to get over your dad."

"Hmm." I'd have to think about that one.

As soon as I got off the phone, I searched the house, and in a box that hadn't been unpacked, I found the book. I pulled it out and haphazardly opened to a passage: *I am entitled to miracles .... You are entitled to miracles because what you are ... and what God is, and because you are one with God.*

I really, really wanted to believe it.

*Let miracles replace all grievances. Recognize the problem so it can be solve*d ... *all problems arise because of separation.*

It explained that the feeling of separation from the oneness of God is what creates all problems. I thought about that feeling I used to have as a child, that invisible, invincible force that protected me. It was a feeling I hadn't had in a long time.

I read on, and the calming voice of the text offered no quick and easy fixer, but it suggested a new path. I wouldn't feel completely free of problems, frustration, or being overwhelmed until I made peace the goal—peace of mind, that is. The problem would be solved when I recognized that my mind is split, like I was holding onto something that just wasn't working. I got it. Just for a second, there was a simple shift.

My relationship with Dick was a relationship without foundation or support beams, collapsing in on itself. Deep down, I knew that I could save myself by walking away into the sunshine and fresh air. I imagined myself simply leaving him.

Chapter Seventeen

*"God's will for me is perfect happiness ...
I can be still an instant and go home."*

The strange thing about California was that it showed me what Dick and our relationship was all about. It shed some light on it. Sunshine, I guess. But better yet, California gave me the opportunity to progress at a much more rapid pace in my career than Rochester would have ever let me.

As much as things were falling apart at home, I was thriving at work. I was winning sales management awards left and right and making more money than before. If it weren't for Dick, I would be having more fun. Management was my thing. I was feeling more competent and confident than ever.

I liked the long hours. Work gave me an excuse not to go home, and I was searching for a new place to live. It would not be long before I was out.

I needed a transfer and to do that I needed to make myself more valuable to the company. Positioning—it came down to bare tactics. I took online management courses when most people were enjoying their weekends. I'd get my hands on anything business-related to make my job easier or better. My burning ambition and intense focus came from my deep desire to be successful. To say to my father, "See? I'm not so dumb after all. I'm a success."

I liked the company I worked for, but LA was not for

me. I had to get out of the city. The traffic and smog clogged my mind, making it hard to find my center. I needed a smaller city that could be my own safe harbor.

In the meantime, I needed to get away from Dick, and that opportunity came from an unexpected place—Pam, to the rescue. She called while I was at the office.

"Hey, Ryley, you're never going to believe it. Chip and I are getting married. I want you to be a bridesmaid."

"No way! Oh, my God—congratulations!" I said.

"Can you believe it?"

"No." But I could; she was destined to be married. Chip Nichols was her perfect, handsome business guy, the one she had been looking for all along.

"Me, either. I am so happy, I could burst."

"Pam. Awesome. You deserve all the happiness out there."

I hadn't seen her since leaving New York, and that was over a year. We e-mailed and kept up, but it wasn't like when I lived in New York. The thrill of hunting for the right man was over for Pam, and I hadn't needed her advice for a while.

"Well, Ryley, I have a little favor to ask, and I know that you might not be able to do it. You're not going to believe it, but I'm having the hardest time getting into one of the Triangle Buildings. You won't believe what's going on with the construction. Beautiful, beautiful architecture. As you walk into their newest building, the lobby ... oh, my God— beautiful! There is imported marble everywhere and fountains to die for. It's like walking into Italy. You know it would be just a perfect place for the wedding pictures, but I can't get anyone to open the building on a Saturday. You have no idea of the nightmare I've been through. For a wedding, can you believe it? I've even tried Hank, but he won't budge, not even for Chip. You know ... he would open it if you called him."

I couldn't believe what she was asking.

I stammered, "You know, Pam, I haven't talked to Hank in the longest time—"

She interrupted, "Oh, Ryley, this is the most important day of my life. I just want it to be perfect. This would mean so much to me. Can't you just call him? There's no harm in just asking. Oh, please, please, please?"

"I don't even have a number for him anymore," I pleaded, trying to lie my way out of it.

"Oh, I have it right here."

It wouldn't matter what I said. I was doomed. So of course, I ended up calling. I called the office line, not his cell, knowing he wouldn't pick up. I made sure to call late, New York time; it was cocktail hour. That way, I could tell Pam I could never get through to him—the perfect excuse.

"Ryley," he greeted me in his opulent voice.

"Uh, yeah," I uttered, as if I had been just hit by a Mack truck and was lying, naked, face up, in front of a million-viewer audience.

"How are you?" His voice was filled with excitement, and it did that thing to me. It did that amazing thing, that spark, and then the heat started at my loins, burned through my stomach, and made its way to my cheeks, leaving my face red and palms sweaty.

God, please make this feeling go away.

"Oh. Hank. Sorry to bother you. I have a friend ... uh, ... who was wondering the craziest thing ... if ... ah ... one of your buildings could be opened for a wedding shoot, on a weekend of all things." I stammered with the complete expectation that he'd just say no.

"Are you coming to the wedding?" he asked.

"What?"

"Are you coming to the wedding?"

"Um ... it's OK. I understand that the buildings should only be open during business hours, liability and all."

"Are you coming to New York?"

"Well, thanks anyway. I guess the building's out of the question."

"I'll be happy to open the building in person. Are you coming?"

"Aren't you still married?"

"Come on ... I want to see you."

I was mortified when I got off the phone. I did not want to talk to Hank and did not want to be in a wedding. I don't know how Pam did it. Practice, I guess—she got me to do both.

To be polite, I asked Dick if he wanted to go and was relieved when he said no. I was going back home on my own.

Chapter Eighteen

"I am not a body. I am free."

The bridesmaid dresses were gross, mafia-Italian types—ruffles from my navel to my forehead. Pam. Pam Polpetta was called "Meatball" in grade school, not because she looked like one but because Polpetta means meatball in Italian—there would be plenty at the reception. Not only did I not want to see Hank, but I also couldn't stand the thought of him seeing me in a purple passion, velvet nightmare. Pam should have had matching bags to cover our heads. I'd been working out and eating a lot less to prepare for this moment. The only good thing about the dress was that it had a built-in corset, which made my boobs look huge and my waist tiny.

On the day of the wedding, I had a cocktail. Pam's family loved to drink, and mini-bars were set up everywhere. I needed something to help me relax and forget about Dick and my terrifying frock. With Dick's micromanagement of my eating, it was impossible to loosen up and have fun when food was around. My closet eating—I mean, car eating—had nothing to do with my unhappiness. Yeah, right.

The icing on the cake would have been if Sarah had been there, but hell doesn't freeze over that easily. Sarah and Pam—oil and vinegar.

Sarah was pissed I had even considered calling Hank for

the space. "She makes you do things you don't want to do!"

"Oh, you mean like yoga? You're just jealous because you're not invited to the wedding."

"You mean you're jealous because I won't have to wear that dress."

At the time of our conversation, I thought she'd gotten that one right. But after sipping my cocktail, I began to change my mind.

I let the alcohol ooze into my bloodstream, making my body feel warm and free. The clear liquid unwound the tension that clenched my heart. I was light and above the clouds, as if the bridesmaid slippers were dancing on tiptoe through the nuptials. Being so far away from Dick was intoxicating in itself; the booze just made it better. Who knew a buzz could make the whole planet love me, or was it me who was loving the planet?

By the time the wedding actually began, I was half in the bag. I had two cocktails but it felt like twenty. My bridesmaid duties were sloppy—I don't think anyone noticed, except for the other bridesmaids, who were probably scoffing at me (they knew better than to drink before the vows). They just didn't get how helpful I was; after all, I was trying to keep things light and fun.

The beginning was a blur and bore. All I could recall was that the music was prerecorded and the vows were unoriginal. Finally, when the I do's were done, the groomsmen escorted us to a black stretch limo with a stocked bar. I helped myself to a glass of champagne and toasted the bride.

Pam hired a makeup artist to touch us up on our way to the photo shoot. Her name was Colby, and she was really good. I looked like a movie star and joked with her, asking how she could fit so much smoke and mirrors into such a small cosmetic case. God, I was funny! I have a tendency to laugh at my own jokes when no one is laughing. I was laughing a lot.

My buzz made me feel like I didn't have a body. A priest once told me we are spirits of God and our bodies are just our shells—"You are so much more than your physical body." I got what he meant. Why couldn't I have felt it all the time, like after eating a full pint of Ben & Jerry's and a half-package of Double Stuf Oreos? I wanted to feel this light when my body felt heavy from food and lethargic from life.

I floated into the Triangle Building, right past Hank. I never saw him standing at the door because the lobby was indeed breathtaking. Hank caught up with me by the fountain, knocking me out with his handsome face. I had forgotten how his smile could bore through my soul. I took a slow breath and was careful, so he wouldn't see the adoration in my eyes. I became polite and reserved.

The edges of my surroundings were still soft and warm from the champagne. Two girls in the wedding party commented on my glow and asked if I were pregnant. Not a chance; it had been close to two months since I'd had uneventful or bad sex with Dick. "What's wrong with you, Ryley? Why can't you relax?" Dick had asked, with a grip too tight on my wrists, digging into me with forceful thrusts. Two minutes later, it was over, and he was downstairs smoking a cigarette and watching television. I'd turned over and tried to go to sleep. Sleep never came fast enough.

The photographer took forever. A million rolls later and after posing—sitting, standing, shoulders in, turned in this direction and that direction—we were getting close to a finish. I was tired of smiling; I needed another drink.

"Ryley, that guy has a major thing for you," said one of the bridesmaids. Hank was staring at me as if someone had bonged him on the head with a frying pan.

The photographer was done, and as I was leaving the building, Hank touched my elbow and whispered, "You look incredible. You are the most beautiful woman here. I have to see you!"

I looked him square in the eye. I mean, I really looked at him. When was he going to stop this game. "Don't you have someone waiting for you at home?"

"Oh, Ryley, there is no marriage. You're the one I want to be with."

"Whatever," I said as I wiggled my elbow out of the palm of his hand. I walked away, and he ran to catch up to me.

"Please, can I see you tonight?" His voice was soft and his face too stunning. Small beads of sweat on his upper lip gave off a hint of desperation.

"Hank. The wedding. Code 4, paragraph 3 in the bridesmaid manual states getting together with a married man who doesn't sit at the head table is not an option."

"After the reception."

"No can do. I leave for California tomorrow, early."

I escaped and walked quickly to the limo before he could say anything else. Once in the limo, I nudged myself between bridesmaids, who were sweaty from the shoot. Their perfume had lost its linger, and their bodies began to smell like salt and vinegar. I poured champagne and joked around with my comrades. Pam, being the good friend that she is, thought I was funny and kept on saying how happy she was to see me. No kidding, really.

Being single with a bunch of girls for a night was fabulous. I danced until my feet were like small water balloons. At one-thirty in the morning, I made my way back to my hotel room. As I reached the door, I heard my phone ringing. I slid the key strip as fast as I could and ran to the telephone. I thought it would be Sarah or maybe even Dick.

"I've been calling all night. I wanna come over."

"Jesus, Hank."

"Ryley, please. I want to see you."

"Listen, Hank. The answer is n-o. Go to bed."

Hank chortled, "OK, so where is he?"

He had a point. I wasn't in the best relationship. Neither was he. Or so he said. I never saw Hank once with a wedding ring; I wondered if he owned one. Was he *really* married, or was it a ploy? I said nothing.

So he continued, "So what do you see in that guy?"

"He knows when to say good-bye ... Hank, it's late. I have to be up early. Have a good night."

I hung up before he could say another word. Keeping him away was hard, but after the pain I'd already been through, I had no choice.

The phone rang two seconds later.

"I'm coming over," he said.

"No, you're not." I hung up on him.

The phone rang again.

"I'm on my way now."

"No!" I yelled into the dead air on the receiver.

Hank did come over. He banged on my door until three in the morning. I let him in, only because he was making so much noise that I was afraid someone had already called the front desk. When he came in, he had only one thing in mind—sex. He put on the charm, thick, but it felt all wrong. I realized I really didn't want him here; I wanted him to leave. I wasn't doing anything with anyone until I had things resolved with Dick. I couldn't just bounce from man to man.

"How can you just come in here when you're with someone else?" I asked him.

But he wouldn't answer. He was in conquer mode. He nudged me toward the bed, trying to get a good grope.

Maybe he sensed I was still attracted to him, but he was beginning to step over the line. He started to be such a jerk— no, more like an absolute asshole. I pushed him away and was about to tell him off when he, too, realized he'd gone too far. He got up, turned into a gentleman, apologized, and gave me his famous smile. He stayed a little longer, and I saw up close, face to face, that this was not the guy I thought he was. He had shown a side of himself that I'd never seen before. He gave me a hug and a chaste peck on the cheek, and then he was gone.

Chapter Nineteen

"I am determined to see things differently."

It's not where you start, it's where you finish. And I was finished. Finished in love.

Back in California, I wanted to crawl out of my skin and scream. I walked in late from flying all day to a house filled with smoke. It wasn't on fire, not yet. Dick had company—the infamous coworker, Mindy, and her decrepit husband, Jack. Jack was older than dirt. Mindy had penciled eyebrows and a high-pitched, childish voice. She was thin and gawky and could barely pull off pretty. They were both chain-smokers, as was Dick, and had already saturated the house in a fog of cigarette smoke. The only fresh air was outside, two miles away.

The thing that made Jack and Mindy tolerable was the fact that they could cook. The kitchen was filled with gourmet delights, appetizers that were shaped into seashells that melted in your mouth and tasted a bit like heaven. That is, if I could taste through all the tar and tobacco. They were making dinner but it wasn't ready yet; it was just before ten o'clock.

"Margarita, anyone?" Jack offered.

The blender whizzed as I sipped on a glass of ice water. I was not interested in drinking. I had had enough at the wedding. I also liked to be sober when Dick was drinking because I never knew what mood his drinking would take him to. The three of them were blitzed. I was hungry following the flight; I hadn't touched my plane food and was looking forward to whatever they were making.

Dinner was served at 11:12. I was so hungry that I was about to start nibbling on our neighborhood dog, Max, who was roaming outside, looking for a place to poop, probably right next to my azaleas.

As I helped Jack bring the food to the table, I noticed Dick touching Mindy's hand and looking at her in an overly affectionate way. She returned the look; I knew it wasn't the first time. Then his hand leisurely made its way to her elbow. It might as well have been her left breast. The flirting continued through the night, and even senior-citizen Jack noticed something askew with his wife. As a sober observer, I watched the blasted trio—it had an interesting way of revealing life in plain view. I lost my appetite, not just because they were falling over one another in a way that would break my heart if I still loved Dick but also because she was so thin, and I felt so fat. Dick hand-fed her while I got the *look* with each bite that said, "Should you really be eating that?"

At 2:48, they left. Dick was drunk.

"Motherfucker!" He had dropped his drink on the tiled kitchen floor, and glass shards were scattered in every corner.

"'Night, Dick, I'm going to bed," I said as I headed for the upstairs guest room. It locked from inside.

"Aren't you gon' to tell me 'bout the weddin'? How was lover boy Hank?" he slurred, as if he had swallowed a pound of marbles.

I turned around before my foot hit the first step. "Excuse me?"

"You know, your lover boy, Mr. Silverspoon!"

I wanted to say, "You should talk." But I knew better than to start a fight, so I said instead, "Good night. It's late."

"So how wuz he?"

I said nothing.

"You had him, di'n't you?"

I still said nothing.

"Hey, bitch, I'm talkin' to you!" His voice was too loud.

I was at the top of the stairs, walking on eggshells. Only a dozen steps to the guest room door.

"You shlut, Ryley … slut-whore …" He was still swearing and stumbling in the kitchen. I was safe inside, with the door locked. Or so I hoped. I whispered one long prayer over and over and nearly peed my pants, I was so nervous. I looked outside the window to see if it was safe to jump if he came crashing in. He was still raging downstairs when I decided that if I jumped from the window, I might land on the front lawn.

He suddenly stopped and turned on the television.

My eyes filled, but I didn't let the tears roll down. God, I hated him. God, I really hated him. How did I get here?

Pain is pain. It doesn't matter where or how you get it—whether you have been sexually abused, abandoned, beaten, violated, victimized, or just stuck with a loser who you thought you could save or somehow love. Pain hurts, and even though it might have different degrees, it still hurts.

—

The good thing about life is when you can't take any more, when you can't take another breath, something shifts.

Without any discussion or warning, five days later, Dick got a vasectomy. I came home from work earlier than usual, and there was Dick in his leather recliner with a bag of frozen peas on his balls. Interesting choice of pain reliever,

I thought. My guess was that he went for something close to his original size.

I had the perfect out. Non-negotiable. Dick knew what family meant to me. We were over.

I finally left him. Why it took so long, I don't know. Sarah says that we choose pain to try to learn things when we can choose joy instead. I had no idea what I'd learned—maybe that I was stupid when it came to loving men. Maybe I'd thought I could have helped Dick, but I finally realized I needed to help myself first.

The truth was that besides Dick being the rebound guy, he was the takeaway close. In sales, when the buyer doesn't want to buy, you take away the sale by saying something like, "Well, this product isn't for you." People want what they can't have. The best way to close something is to take it away. Dick was something I could never have, never have his unconditional love and acceptance. He was my hardest sale. So it took forever, but I finally walked away.

On a day when he was on a business trip, I packed up all my belongings and moved into a townhouse close to my office. I could hear the blood in my ears pounding as I packed. I was so worried he would come home at any minute.

The movers were quick. I paid them to be. Most of the furniture in his house was mine so the truck was full as it rolled down the driveway. His place was left looking bare, enormous, and full of dust bunnies. I'd planned the move for weeks prior to his trip. As each day came closer to my exit date, I prepared more and more to move on with my life and get away from him. I left without remorse.

The sad part was that the five-thousand-plus-square-foot home I left behind would be something I could never afford on my own. I'd miss the nights in the Jacuzzi and the pool and the lush lawns. He benefited from the upgrades that I provided for his home: the landscaping, hardscaping, custom window treatments, and down payment. I wouldn't see that money from him; it would've been enough to provide me a comfortable new beginning. It wasn't worth losing sleep over. I knew I could save for a new nest egg with the job that I had. But more importantly, I got my freedom back, which was priceless. Oh, yeah, and I still had an engagement ring that would easily turn into cash.

—

Chapter Twenty

"The peace of God is shining in me now"

Dick never called. The feeling must have been mutual.

My company was willing to relocate me anywhere in California, so after a few months in a rented townhouse and checking out my options, I found the place I wanted to call home. It had been one year that I had lived in L.A. and close to two years that I had been with Dick. It was about time I moved on. I took the relocation package and moved to San Diego.

The city was unfamiliar, and I was homesick, so I called Toad a lot. I would have called Pam too but she had vanished into married life.

"Well, what's it like?" Sarah asked.

"All I do is stumble around trying to get my bearings. I feel lost."

"Describe the place."

"It's a coastal city with lots of stucco. There are continuous mega-clusters of McMansions, two trillion homes trying not to look like each other, but all look the same."

In North County these prefabricated stucco homes were tightly packed together on lots the size of postage stamps. Almost all the homes were similar in shape, color, and size. Then I explained to her that the southern part of the city bordered Mexico and had deep Hispanic roots. Unlike LA, this was a sleepy community with lots to do. For me, the coast was the most gratifying, but I had no one to share it with. "I don't know anyone. Do you think I made a wrong decision?"

"Give it time, Rye. Go out for a run or a bike ride or rent Rollerblades. Do all the things that you can't do here in winter, and let me know about it and make me jealous. Then you'll start to feel better."

So I took her advice but rented a bike instead of Rollerblades because I didn't want to kill myself. There was a twenty-mile path along the bay. The water glimmered, and the sun was so bright, it burst beams of light through the flawless blue sky. Maybe I could get used to perfect days, cool breezes, warm sun, and no pollution.

The best part was the quality and pace of life. Everything was slower, even the service at the best restaurants, which took time getting used to. But the food was so good and the tropical paradise setting was so soothing. I was still working hard, but I was learning to slow down and play.

I checked out the museums and parks. Balboa Park was huge—green grounds that never ended, filled with century-old eucalyptus and melaleuca trees. You could spend months in the park and still not see everything. There were over two dozen buildings that housed museums of some sort, like the Museum of Art, the Museum of Man, the Museum of History, the Aerospace Museum, the Museum of Trains, and the Museum of Science–Ruben H. Fleet (the IMAX theater was the best). And there were other attractions, like Globe Theatre and the San Diego Zoo. I checked them out on my own until I found friends to play with.

In San Diego, I could get in shape by just playing outside. My new coworkers filled the gap, teaching me how to play beach volleyball. On Friday's after work, a group would go to Del Mar, where the stretch of sand was endless. San Diego smelled like sunshine and ocean mists—not the deep seaweed ocean smells of the Northeast but light, fresh, and salty.

Every beach had its own personality and charms. Moonlight Beach was the beach to boogie board or run at low tide. Any beach was where I wanted to be when I wasn't working; there were so many to choose from that I hadn't picked a favorite yet. Too much fun to be had—from Jet Skiing on the bay, to boating, to hiking in the nearby mountains, to theater and great restaurants—the choices were limitless. It would take a lifetime to run out of activities, especially with weather so perfect. The days were all the same: sunny, seventies, and blue skies, and I was beginning to get used to it. In fact, I was beginning to love it.

"Toad, you're not going to believe this place!"

"I knew it was only a matter of time."

I met Paige at the San Diego Business Executives Charter, and she introduced me to a few bachelors. The networking mixers were the best place to meet guys. They were great rebound men, who either loved to surf or go to movies. They helped me feel good about myself again. Nothing serious came from the handful of dates. I was happy to be free and uncommitted.

The truth was, I was done looking for Prince Charming. I had stopped believing in a man on a white horse who could fulfill my needs. There was too much pressure in that. It came down to me. I still had small holes inside myself and wanted to feel whole on my own.

The heartbeat of San Diego lent itself to warm sunsets. Bookstores and coffee houses sat in pockets of the city, making my new surroundings charming and cozy. It was easy to settle into a city with so many delightful streets that had interesting nooks to explore. But as the holidays approached, I began feeling nostalgic for home and decided to go to New York for Christmas to see family and Sarah.

Toad had been out of town during Pam's wedding, and we never got to catch up face to face. Now I could. My parents' house was full at Christmas, so they were cool when I asked to stay at Sarah's during my visit. If I stayed with my family, there would be too many questions about breaking off the engagement and moving to San Diego, and why hadn't I filled out the applications for grad school, and here is a flier for adult ballet in your area. I loved my family, but I could only take the abuse in small doses.

My first day in New York, I ran into him. Hank. I was at the grocery store, picking up a fruit basket before going to my parents' house. We hadn't been in touch since that night after Pam's wedding.

"Ryley?"

I looked up from the large selection of colorful and tastefully displayed fruit baskets and was surprised. The dumb look on my face confirmed it. I wondered how fat I looked.

"Hi," I said. He looked incredible, as usual, in his gray cashmere sweater and white shirt, layered beneath the chocolate-brown bomber jacket, with leather gloves peeking out of the left pocket. His face was clean shaven and just right.

"What are you doing here?" he asked.

"Oh, I'm here for the holidays." He touched my shoulder as if to give me a hug. I pulled away slowly; his touch was too much. I could feel the blood surging into my cheeks. I hoped he couldn't tell.

"Not wearing your engagement ring?" he remarked with a raised eyebrow.

"Oh, it didn't work out," I said, looking around for his

wife. I looked down at his hand. "I notice you're still not wearing yours either, Hank."

He smiled.

"Ryley, can we get together while you're here?"

His face was touchable. "Ah, I don't know," I answered, even though I was interested. I was now single and unattached. I wished he were, too.

"Oh, come on. Where are you staying? We could go out for a bite or a hike in Mendon Ponds Park. I know you're an outdoor fan." As he spoke, I noticed his cheeks were flushed and his pupils dilated. Was he nervous?

"You know, I really gotta get going." I looked at my watch and put down the fruit basket. My parents wouldn't mind my coming home empty-handed; they just wanted me home. I headed toward the exit.

"Oh, come on," he said.

I picked up my pace.

"Please?" He was following me.

I twirled around and said, "You know, I don't think that's a good idea. Aren't you still with Elizabett?"

"Ryley, I want to see you. Friends? Let's catch up. It's been too long, baby."

Baby. Where did that come from? It came from his unmistakable charm that made me forgive him.

"I'm staying at Sarah Toadvine's," I uttered over my shoulder, as I continued walking out of the store.

—

I arrived at my parents' home, sans fruit basket. After a day of hugs, warmth, and gentle inquiries about my weight, grad school, and a Dick-less life, I escaped to Toad's.

I knocked on Sarah's door and walked right in before

she could answer. She came barreling down the hall and attacked me with a hug. It was amazing that such a small body had so much force. It had been too long, but it also felt like it was only yesterday since I'd seen her.

"God, I have so much to tell you! But you first," Sarah said, all smiles.

"I have nothing new to report. You go."

"OK, come in, come in," she said as she dragged me with one hand, suitcase in the other. We went back to her tiny kitchen. She was making jasmine tea for us and had cut an apple into boats that rocked on a plate in the center of the kitchen table. The winter night was dark and gloomy, like the rest of the day had been—typical Rochester weather.

"Uncle Blake was in town."

"What!" I almost screamed. Blake was Sarah's mother's older brother who lived in Texas and never came to Rochester to visit. I had never met him, just seen pictures.

"Yep, he stopped over unannounced when I was having dinner at my parents'."

"You have to be kidding," I said, almost breathless.

"Nope. And you're never going to believe it—it was so cool."

"What do you mean, it was cool? Are you high?"

"Nope."

"Would you please spill the beans?!"

"All right already. One or two?" she said, pointing to the green jasmine tea bags.

"Jesus!"

"OK, one then." She plopped a single bag into the pot. "Well, we were all eating. Mom hadn't finished her first martini at that point. My dad was in two, and then the doorbell rang and there he was."

"Yeah, and?" I wished she'd hurry up and tell the story.

"It was fine."

"What do you mean, it was fine?"

"I can't tell you what my mother said, but she wouldn't let him in. For the first time, it was like she was doing something, and it has made it easier to forgive her. He doesn't scare me anymore. I know that I can move on."

"Are you nuts?"

"No, really, it's OK. Don't get me wrong—there was a time when I would have loved to have seen my mother have him arrested, but it doesn't matter anymore."

I couldn't breathe; I was in shock. I remembered everything. I knew about Blake and couldn't see how she could say what she was saying. It seemed like yesterday when Sarah told me.

It was the summer Sarah turned eleven. Blake was living in Rochester back then. He was a handsome man with thick blonde hair and a sharp nose. Like Sarah's mom, he had good bone structure. Dashing.

The sky was a clear blue on the day he cornered Sarah, not with physical force but through manipulation. He knew how much she loved to sail. His forty-foot wooden Concordia yawl was the prize in his scheme. That's how he got her alone. He took her out on the water, where he raped her, right on the foredeck, over and over, scraping off her clothes, leaving fingernail scratches on her throat and wrists. Her screams could not be heard; they were too far off. When he was done, he brought her back to shore, after the Yacht Club had closed tight for the night.

He was too smart to let her go home the way she was. He conveniently had a change of clothes tucked away in the trunk of his Mercedes sedan. And when she was done cleaning herself up and changing her clothes, he told her to never speak a word about what had happened or he would come after her and kill her; it was as if he were driving nails into her coffin.

"How could you forgive such a monster?"

She said, "If I didn't, he would still own me. I had to let him go."

Sarah's mother knew what had gone on with Uncle Blake. Sarah didn't even have to tell her. She was all too familiar with the looks Blake had given her young daughter. They were the same looks that he had given her when she was a child, so many years before.

If she'd ever regretted letting her child be alone with him, Sarah never knew about it.

"How can you just forgive your mom for what she did? She never helped you. She was never there for you. How does a mother do that?" I asked.

"She did the best she knew how to do."

"What on earth do you mean?"

"I have forgiven them but not for their benefit. I did it for mine. And when you truly forgive someone, you will get it. It's not like it just happened. I've been working on this moment for years. He hasn't been by the house since we were in high school. This time, it was different, not only because my mom was different but because I'm different."

"How can you just do that?"

"That's just it. I'm not 'just' doing it; it's been a process. But if I'm in a situation like I was in just a few days ago, where I saw his face like that, I know that I can handle it. God, I feel so free."

"I don't get it. You wouldn't have him arrested?" I asked awkwardly.

"You know, I already tried that. He's got a mark on his record, but it was his word against mine. Rye, you don't get it, my work is done. I am free of him."

I was in awe of Sarah, completely and utterly in awe of her, because I believed her. I believed she could do such a remarkable thing. It's who she was. Astonishing. It's just that I couldn't. I had the fingerprint of my father's rage in me, and if I were Sarah I would hate Blake. Hate him until the day he died.

Sarah saw my face, read my thoughts, and said, "You don't get it. Letting go so you can move on is through forgiveness. You become tortured and stuck when you can't forgive. It's the key to happiness. Like the *Course* says, if you are willing … if you are willing to forgive in that willingness, something opens up in you and shifts. And that shift gets greater the more you practice learning to forgive, and then a miracle happens: You find the key to happiness. You find peace."

"My God, Sarah, what on earth are you talking about?"

"When you push away the fear and are willing to forgive, miracles happen. I'm telling you, I know what I am talking about here! You just have to be willing."

"What happened to you?"

"No, Rye, what happened to *you*? When did you become so hard and lost? You can't please your dad by showing him that you can make a bunch of money. The whole idea is to get to a place where you're not depending on anything external, like his approval. Find peace in your heart and head and maybe he'll be able to see the real you—or maybe he won't, but you will know who you are, instead of someone stuck and lost."

"Ha-ha, yeah, right."

"Ryley, I mean it. Think about it."

"Hm-m-m …."

Chapter Twenty-One

"This instant is the only time there is."

The next morning in Sarah's kitchen, I sipped coffee out of a bowl-like cup. The hot brown liquid made its way down my throat, warming and calming me on the cold, wintry day. I sat peacefully in the breakfast nook as the heat of the cup warmed my hands. Sarah groggily walked in her pajamas. Her hair rumpled around her face.

"Morning," she said in a sleepy voice.

"Hey, you. I made coffee."

I loved the way she still had bed-sheet crinkles on her face. She slept hard, sinking into her bedding like a satellite falling to earth. I wanted to talk about what she told me yesterday. But every time I'd go back to the topic, she'd say, "Let it go" or "Drop it," like I didn't get something, like I was speaking in a foreign language. So I did, even though it nagged at me.

"It smells great," she said as she poured herself a cup of coffee in the same type of mug and made her way to a seat beside me. She went on, "You know, I've been thinking."

"Yeah?"

"What if Hank was your what-if man?"

"What?"

"You know ... maybe he's the guy we all have, where we ask ourselves, 'What if something were different?' You know, the guy you wonder if he's the right soul mate? Should I have let him go? If you gave it another chance, would it be right? Would we still be together. *You* know … the one you still dream about."

I gave her a blank look. "You're kidding, right? He's married."

She looked up from her coffee. "Is he?" She hesitated. "If he calls, you might get together and be sure. Make sure there are no regrets. You don't want to be old and gray and still be wondering."

I took her advice.

He picked me up on Saturday morning. The air was crisp, and there was a two-inch layer of crusty snow on the ground. We had no plan, other than to go cruising through the countryside and end up at Mendon Ponds Park, a good place to hike. I went with no expectations, just sheer excitement and curiosity.

Even with all the time that had gone by since the first day we met, he could still cause a lump of sand in my throat and make my heart beat like a chased rabbit. I thought I was over him. Apparently not.

He picked me up in a new silver Range Rover, the kind with the bubble-eye front lights. He looked preppy and rugged—same bomber jacket, with a thick wool sweater, corduroys, and Maine gum boots.

The first thing I noticed when I climbed into the car was the music—the same songs from my bedroom, years ago. Bryan Ferry's melodic, haunting voice swept me away, as if time and space had stopped.

The velvet rhythms made our journey dreamlike, as if the countryside were a backdrop. Music could do that. It made me feel things I normally was incapable of feeling. It took down the veil between illusion and reality and blended them. We cruised around in our secluded capsule, everything in slow motion, the air trancelike. The words stumbled out of my mouth. "Are you really married?"

"Realistically, no. Legally, yes. You're my reality. Things are going to change. I'm going to leave her."

I didn't believe him.

"I'm coming out to California," he said resolutely.

I laughed. "Of course you are."

"Seriously, Ryley, I will be in California within the year. Mark my words. I just have to finish closing these two deals."

He went on to tell me about the two buildings he had the exclusives on and was in the middle of leasing. The commission was more than four hundred thousand dollars, more commission than I had ever seen. There was always something stuck between us.

I stared outside, letting the scenery roll frame by frame outside my window. The suburbs had faded into frozen fields and farmland. I noticed straggling leaves barely clinging to branches and icy snow wedged in the nooks of trees.

"Hank, you'll never leave her, and you're not moving to California. And even if you did, it would be too late. By then, I'd already have found someone. It's OK. I mean it's really OK. It's not in the cards for us; if it was, it would have already happened. Let's just enjoy each other's company today and leave it alone."

He pulled off the road. We were at Mendon Ponds Park. I spotted an orange-brown leaf still clinging to a maple tree. In front of us were pine trees neatly covered in white snow, as if they were made of gingerbread and lightly sprinkled with powdered sugar. There seemed to be six more inches of snow at the park than at Sarah's home, and the snow was softer and more inviting. I gazed outside the window, taking it all in. When Hank softly pulled at my arm, I turned to look at him.

His eyes penetrated. "You don't understand; I'm coming to California … for you."

I looked away. He leaned closer to me. "Just don't get married. And if you have to, you must promise me you'll call me … so I can run down the aisle and stop it."

I looked into his eyes. "It's only in Episcopal churches and in movies that you can object at a wedding. And it's not about giving an ex-boyfriend a final chance to crash the wedding. It's purely a legal question, to see if there's a pre-existing marriage license. Really, objecting at a wedding doesn't do anything. You know, you might be as handsome as a movie star but you're—"

He laughed, and then cupped my face in his large hand and gently kissed my forehead. "Wait for me. I'll be there."

It was a magnificent game that we played.

His hand swept over my face like Hershey's syrup, slow and sweet. He pulled me over to him and gently touched below my shoulder blade, raising my arm to guide the sleeve of my jacket off my shoulder. Like magic, my jacket was off and what was left behind was his warm palm in the center of my back, guiding me to his lips. The car windows grew a thin layer of fog. I pulled away and suggested a walk.

Outside, the air was cold and sharp. When I exhaled, my breath turned into a white plume. A trail led off to the right. Where we parked, the ground was heavy in snow. The strong and fragrant smell of burning cedar was in the air from a farmhouse chimney across the street. There's nothing like dry, cold air hitting your face, turning cheeks rosy, biting your throat and lungs. I felt clean and light inside.

Winter was alive. Hank hit the back of my shoulder with

a snowball. I turned and retaliated. We scooped the snow and tossed it without forming balls; the spray of snow was light. Our bodies fell to make snow angels. We rolled into snow banks, flapping arms and legs.

And then Hank scooped me up and gave me a piggyback ride. I felt small and free. The winter air blew cold through my hair as he raced down the trail toward the closest pond. Our playing like children was pure, encompassed in the moment, wanting to be nowhere else.

After hours in the woods, climbing trees, hiking, and sledding on our backs like otters, we made our way back to the car, wet and frozen to the bone.

It wasn't the blasting heat from the car that warmed us; it was us. It started with his kiss on the inside of my wrist, the soft spot. Slow. His manner suggested barely suppressed energy. Then it was the kiss behind my ear and then we were making out again.

When we finally arrived at Sarah's house, it was beginning to get dark. Once in her driveway, Hank reached back to the seat behind him and gave me a pale-orange polo shirt. It was folded into a perfect square.

"Here, I want you to have this."

It was the only thing of his that he ever gave me.

"I'll walk you up." He reached for the door handle.

"I think I got it from here," I said with a smile.

After dashing into the house, I sank my face, little by little, into the shirt and inhaled. It smelled of him. I wore that shirt every night for as long as I could, never washing it until his scent was gone, overwhelmed by mine.

I still have it.

Chapter Twenty-Two

"All fear is past and only love is here."

I arrived back in San Diego with the effervescent bubbles of Hank's charm dissipating like club soda going flat. Feeling lonely and frustrated in the love department, I poured myself into work, back to long hours and working weekends. It was easy to be a workaholic.

Then, a few months after my return, the impossible happened. The impossible on the East Coast happened, that is—I was promoted to director of sales and marketing. If I were still in New York, it would have taken a lot longer, an MBA at Harvard, and a ton more campaigning to be in the management position. In the New York that I came from, they didn't hand over big jobs to pip-squeaks who had been in the business fewer than ten years. Working your ass off and being good at what you do doesn't warrant such a big promotion. But Californians were different, more entrepreneurial, and they liked people who worked hard. They'd give anyone a chance. California was the epicenter of job opportunities, with an open-minded and relaxed business style, less ivory tower management, and more capitalist entrepreneurs. It was easy for me to make money in the Golden State. Californians understood me more than I understood myself.

The place began to feel like home. Home—a place where

people remembered my name and snippets of my life and were nice enough to inquire. "Hey, Ryley, how was the business trip? Did you get any running in?" or "Hi, Ryley. Your usual *New York Times* and a tall mocha latté? Where've you been? I haven't seen you at the gym?" How could so many strangers know me? Only in California was it possible to have people warm up so quickly.

This strange land reminded me that I was alive again, likeable and friend-worthy. God, it was always so damn gorgeous outside. It was as if the sky let out a big yawn, exhaling a palate of blues, from peacock feather to cerulean and indigo, and occasional clouds so puffy and soft, they made me want to bring them to my face and sink into them slowly. Warm yellow flower buds danced in the wind, bobbing softly to the cadence of the blowing air. It was as if each plant were lit from within. I questioned how nature could be so overpowering that it didn't seem real, as if a painting on the wall were real and nature was not.

More and more, I found myself gravitating toward long stretches of beach where the crash of each wave made its way into the cleft of my cluttered mind. My tense body would ease, freeing and nourishing my spirit and making me feel whole and balanced. Nature did amazing things for me. I took the time to let it in, experiencing sunsets as if for the first time. The beaches would give way to magnificent scenery, a breathless, moving sculpture of natural color. I drew in the radiance of the burning sun, the colors like an overripe peach, slipping into the ocean, leaving behind liquid gold.

The beach felt like coming home. My toes sank deep into the gushy sand, and my nose tingled from the evaporating salty air. I felt small there, protected by something big. I began to embrace nature and God as one. The hurtling waves and the bits of driftwood on the shoreline reminded me of Maine when I was a kid.

Summers in Maine. It was heaven … a place where I could roam free and play make-believe under a birch, fir, or spruce. The sweetest smell was the air—a mixture of salty ocean and syrupy pine. The ocean mist wasn't light like the Californian ocean; it was heavy with seaweed and lobster and clam. We would swim on the east shore of the island because it had a natural cove and the water was calm, creating a perfect natural swimming pool. The North Atlantic water was freezing. The kids on the island would drop ice cubes off the main dock to see how long they would take to melt. On a good day, they would hardly melt, and our lips and fingers would turn blue from the frigid water. Driftwood was plentiful, and every now and then, large logs would roll onto the shore. They became our sea horses. We rode the logs, pretending the wood hobble was our own personal steed.

When we walked through the moss-covered paths to the east shore banks, we'd see toppled scrap driftwood clusters with a single log protruding. To the adult or novice eye, it would appear like a woody mess, but we saw our horses in their stables.

Getting in touch with the good memories of my child-hood gave me the confidence to go forward in my life. I worked hard at work and on myself and soon found that I was prospering in both.

The best news of all was my new salary increase. At least I could buy a house on my own in California. After spending time in many different areas in San Diego, it wasn't hard to know exactly where I wanted to live.

The community I chose was Mission Hills. It was close to downtown and had bungalow and craftsman-style homes that were older than goldfish. The area had nuggets of gold, homes that were built in the 1920s that had good bones. You could find teeny-tiny houses with mahogany floors, original crown molding, and leaded glass or bay windows. These were homes with charm, not cookie-cutter designs. Although these jewels weren't cheap, with a good realtor I was able to find a fixer-upper in my price range. The big hassle was that so did eight other prospective buyers.

Of course, people were lined up to buy the perfect house, which was only minutes from work and the beach and also had a view of the bay from upstairs. Of course, I was last on the list for the house that had the coolest gym within running distance. I had to keep more than my fingers and toes crossed—I crossed my legs and eyes and did the sign of the cross over my chest and prayed.

My mind wandered, meandered, and rambled away from the tasks at hand at work. I could be in a board meeting, looking straight at the person speaking, but I was really placing all my furniture in each room. I was picking out paint colors in my head when I met with the head of engineering. Or while dealing with one of my employees, I was thinking about the right cabinets and countertops for the kitchen.

My prayers were working; the list of prospective buyers was getting shorter and shorter. Possible candidates were dropping like flies from one kind of contingency or another. I'd speed-dialed my realtor, checking on the status, and then, finally, I was at the top of the list. One of our company's attorneys, a nice, quiet man, coached me through the closing and negotiations. He and his wife were the first people I had over when the deal was done, and I was home, in my new house.

You could find my new home nestled at the end of a cul-de-sac in a neighborhood with mature trees. It was just past a sagebrush-covered canyon. The tiny front yard had landscaping that was tropically lush and verdant for such a small space, like a baby garden with accents of whimsical color. Orange and purple birds of paradise framed the small cottage-like house; lantana and daisy-like bushes were tastefully placed throughout the small yard. My favorite plants were soft and low shrubs with thin, green leaves and dozens of periwinkle flowers with yellow centers. Crimson, white, and yellow flowers cascaded from two window boxes on the first floor.

In the back was a small patio, large enough to place a table and canvas umbrella. The patio walls were encased in clinging ivy and bougainvillea that needed a continuous trim. In the southern corner was enough room for a little fountain. Beds of lavender, day lilies, and peonies lined the opposite wall. This was the lavender that I dried and occasionally made sachets to fill the pockets of my clothes and linen cabinet.

After arriving home from a late night at the office, I would light up my sanctuary of a back patio with votive candles. A steady gurgling and tricking from the Italian fountain that hung on the wall added to the peace and calm I found there.

My home was the perfect size for me—three small bedrooms and two tiny baths, all amounting to a mere 1,340 square feet. I liked my walls in close, so I could nestle in the nooks and crannies like a second skin. There were wall-to-wall mahogany hardwood floors, covered by the oriental rugs from my parents' home. These were the same rugs that I had walked on as a child. My mom has a thing for oriental rugs; she collects them like seashells at the beach. The first thing I did before moving in was to paint the stark, white walls a soft, creamy khaki ("taupe sage"), a new favorite that instantly warmed the house and gave it a sophisticated look.

My furniture fit in snuggly, and with custom window coverings, a fox-hunting oil painting, and my endless shelves of books, the place looked great.

My favorite haven was the little living room. It housed a new overstuffed down sofa, which perched in front of a river-stone fireplace. My hoards of blue and white pillows made the sofa inviting for a good book or nap. On the mantelpiece were family photos and pictures of Toad and me. On cool nights in the fall and winter, I would burn dried eucalyptus that would crackle and pop, sending a healing aroma.

This was the room where I began to quiet my restless mind and soul and nurture my spirit. I started to find the time to build a fire or light candles and curl up with the many books that Sarah had given me over the years. They began to calm me down after another day at work. Or I found myself reading magazines with articles on reducing stress with a cup of herbal mint tea in a handmade ceramic mug.

More often than not, when I sat down to read, I nestled in my pillows with the soft light of candles. When I especially needed a calm voice or a healing hand, *A Course in Miracles* would find its way to my lap, as if magically sent by wings.

Peace surrounds me where I go. Peace goes there with me. I'd read a bit and then muse about the meaning of the words, letting their wisdom sink in. I thought about work, about my father, about not absorbing the hurt or worry, about letting go. I began to observe and experience the world from a centered, peaceful place—a place that was mine. Not always but more and more, this was a place I could find or return to.

I began to melt into the words. Maybe the book wasn't so bad after all. I left it out where I'd see it in passing, picking it up and reading a line here and there. This wasn't a crash course. It was a process. As usual, Sarah had been right, and I was overwhelmed with the gratitude of our friendship.

That was the one thing missing in my life in California—Sarah. So, early one evening, I decided to ask for what I wanted and called her.

Sarah picked up the phone after the third ring.

"Hey, how's the house?" was the first thing she asked.

"It would be better if you moved out here and were sipping tea with me right now. Toad, move to California."

"You move back."

"I can't move back to New York. I like the idea that I can make it out here."

"Oh, come on."

"No, I'm serious. This is the dream: I'm a hotshot in corporate America. You know … I started planning for this in ninth grade. Come on; everything that you like is out here."

"Oh, please, you and your job. I don't know."

"Come on, you're more Californian than the natives."

She laughed.

"Rochester is filled with old and bad memories. Give your life a new chance. Fresh start under the sun. The truth is, I miss you too much. You're too far away. Please!"

"I grew up here. It's home to me."

"I know. That's the problem. C'mon … you'll love it here. They have a juice bar on every corner."

"Well, now you have a point!"

Chapter Twenty-Three

"A happy outcome to all things is for sure."

Not every day was a good one.

There were mornings when I awoke with my heart stuck in my throat. I was depressed—not suicidal depressed, but out of sync. Sure, I had the title at work, and the people at the coffee cart knew my name and order, and those at the gym were friendly, but I missed the deep connectedness that comes from being around someone who really knew me. Someone who got me. Surrounded by smiling faces, I was lonely. Nothing real was happening in my life—nothing outside of work.

Sarah's intuition found me. She called my cell, catching me at work, as usual. "Hey, what's up? You are always at work. I'm starting to worry about you."

"I'm in a funk."

"What happened to the girl who likes to get out and play?"

"She's buried under a stack of contracts."

"Do something meaningful and you will feel better."

"Like feeding starving children in Africa or saving the rain forests, like you?"

"Nah. Just be grateful for your life, your breath, your arms, legs, nice earlobes, great eyebrows, clothes, food, and people who love you. Snap out of it. Go play."

"Hey, listen. I gotta go. Another call."

"Call me back," she demanded.

But I didn't call her back. I was haunted by the questions I knew Sarah would ask if I called her back, like, "If you come into this world alone and leave alone, what do you need to do to fill the space in between with some type of meaning?" Nothing came to mind. Even the self-help books that found their way into my life couldn't save me.

I stopped going out and doing things with people. My California friends would make me feel better for the moment, but I felt out of sync and being with them was only a distraction from the suffocating emptiness of my own life.

It was a deep funk.

So once again, I poured myself into work, like a waterfall spilling into a deep pool, and the momentum of my survival continued on.

Okay, work wasn't going well and that was part of the problem. The company was fine with the job I was doing. But I was just so swamped, I was barely treading water. On a Tuesday morning, before the sun was up, I slipped out from under my warm covers and went into the office. I thought that if I got in the office before six, I'd get ahead of the mounting pile on my desk. Wrong.

It was just another typical crazy day; too many things happened at once. As soon as I finished one thing, a new pile showed up. It seemed like the more I did, the more I had to do. Work had always been a steady pulse for me. Even during intense times there was a rhythm of surviving and accomplishment and order. But what was hitting my desk these days was chaotic and overwhelming. I wanted my warm bed back. It was too late to call in sick—as if I'd ever called in sick—I was already there.

The phone rang off the hook, there were eighty-seven

new e-mails, thirteen of which were urgent, and it was only eight-thirty. Why were there so many people in early? Shouldn't they just be getting in? I was the one who wanted to get ahead. Couldn't everyone just stop what they were doing so I could get some work done? It was too early to feel like the day should be over. I was stuck in limbo.

There I sat behind my desk, the phone pressed to my ear, listening to an annoying, coarse voice droning on about why she couldn't help with a customer crisis. It wasn't her job, she was too busy, and it wasn't really the company's problem. My blood pressure was rising and my patience wearing thinner with each grating excuse. The person on the line gave me every reason, motive, and cause why she wouldn't help with the issue. It wasn't her job; it was the customer's problem. She was the third person I'd talked to, and no one wanted to take ownership. All I wanted to do was help the poor customer and get the problem resolved, and then I could move on to the ninety-seven other headaches in front of me.

Finally, I was forwarded to the person who should have taken care of this before it hit my desk. She was the boss of the clerk who was originally not helping the customer. Another Mrs. Dumb Fuck. The customer had gone to her to no avail. "Sorry, can't help you" was her mantra.

It was the theme of the day.

I couldn't put my finger on it. I walked into the office each day, determined to be optimistic. But in a nanosecond, I was stressed. How could I bring my own peace with me when I was spending so much time trying to get other people to just do their jobs? I started to use my self-help tools, hoping to find calm and be fully present. I'd walk like a tortoise to the front door of the office, making sure to listen to the birds before I took my first step in the building. Or I'd breathe deeply, making sure to inhale extra-large gulps of fresh sky before entering the building and being stifled by the recycled and recirculated stale air.

I was sucked into a vortex of inane and anxiety-ridden stupid issues. There was some kind of emergency every day; there was always a fire or crisis—the sales reps' commissions were screwed up, an overblown customer complaint, a contract was going south because of a bad installation. It wasn't just normal problems; it was normal problems on incest.

Every day brought the same state of chaos: a new problem, same personalities. There was no reason to have so many escalations to do the business at hand. Even within the company, departments were at war, and no one was taking responsibility.

I attempted to stay calm. Even though I had a hunch about who was poisoning the brew, I couldn't do anything about it—yet.

My personal strategy for peace of mind was not conventional; much of it came from Sarah, in a care package labeled "Emergency Kit–911." My office was now filled with music from a portable CD player that made sounds of babbling brooks, ocean surf, and monks chanting. Aromatherapy candles came in bulk, with a lot of essential oil bottles— tons of lavender oil—that Toad told me it was the best for calming stress. But the most desperate tactic was the magic wand. She bought it in the dress-up section of a toy store, where tiaras and bright pink boas were hanging from fairy costumes.

The wand was silver with stars and moons dangling from the top. It released glitter when shaken. Sarah told me to wave the wand over my speaker phone during those conference calls that accomplished nothing but endless ego-chatter. I took to waving it whenever I was stuck on the phone with people who were stressed, frustrated, and angry. I tapped that thing a lot and often tapped so hard that people on the call would ask what the noise was. At first I was amused by the wand, and it would lighten my mood to imagine how the person on the other end of the line would respond. But the energy would not shift or make all bad things disappear. It didn't work. Nothing changed. The tension and the lack of solution that went beyond Band-Aids was too much for Sarah's wand and too much for me.

I'd leave the office drained, no miracles in sight, and arrive again the next morning, trying to keep myself together.

I was back in the office on Thursday, sipping on my favorite mocha latté, buried under paperwork, e-mails, and phone calls. I looked at my watch to see that I had twenty-five minutes to prepare for my next meeting. It was our quarterly staff meeting to review our status and go over projections for the year.

When the meeting time came, I was late—a first. I crept into the room, where my eyes met those of my boss, Eric. He gave me the pissed-off face that said, "Be on time next time. We are all busy; what's wrong with you?" I nodded and made my way to an open seat at the conference table.

The first presenter of the day was the vice president of human resources, Dan (not the man; rather a natural snoresville presenter, who forgot to pass out toothpicks to keep our eyelids open). His voice made heads bob and sway. I thought of him as Dracula or Respirator Breath, depending on my mood, because of the breath-sucking way in which he spoke. He was a vain Dracula. I kept catching him glimpsing at his reflection in the glass windows. I don't know what he liked more—checking out his sideburns or hearing himself drone on and on about nothing. The guy had no style and worst of all, he stank—literally. On a bad day he smelled like a dog who'd tangled with a skunk. This was a very bad day.

The next presenter was the vice president of operations, Stan, another Einstein, whom I nicknamed Mr. ZerO, (*O* standing for operations). Unlike Dan, he had no hair, was short, and sported a pot belly that was emphasized by the too-tight shirt button above his black plastic belt. In his piercing twang, he made excuses for not having handouts. He read his presentation off a Post-it note. To stay alert during his presentation I made a game of seeing how often he used the words "service compatibility"—I stopped counting after eleven. I think he was looking for someone to give him the definition.

ZerO was taking his well-practiced ability to whine, "The workload is overwhelming, my staff's overworked, and we can't keep up with the installations." I wanted to interject and say, "Hey, no problem, we'll just stop selling so you can catch up." But I really wanted to ask, "Oh, by the way, ZerO, how's the handicap?" This was Eric's right-hand man at the golf course. Neither was available for customer calls or customer relations. They were too busy attending Tiger Woods' boot camp.

Operations was the reason our company was deteriorating. ZerO couldn't implement an installation if he had a gun to his head. He was too stupid. Brown-nosing went a long way with Eric, and ZerO was so good at it that he used Eric's belly button as a periscope.

Operations already had the largest staff in the company. ZerO just had no idea how to use the resources he had, and he was too busy golfing to bother finding out. Eric wasn't beyond returning the favor. He nodded intently as ZerO lamented his lack of staff. "We need to hire more in fulfilling operations; we don't have enough people. Sales promises customers the impossible." Eric never stepped in when ZerO was playing the blame game; he just left it alone.

My mind started to drift with the next presentation. My index finger slowly traced the rim of my water glass; my eyes meandered around the conference room, as if seeing it for the first time. It was a handsome room on the eleventh floor with high ceilings. The corporate furnishings were old-money conservative—an ostentatious inlaid mahogany conference table, overstuffed leather furniture, and crystal glasses on the credenza opposite the window. But it was the view that was most spectacular.

The drapes were usually closed because the light caused a glare on the digital whiteboard in the front of the room, but since no one was using it today, the drapes were open. What was revealed was an astonishing view. The long sweep of the Coronado Bridge; blue, blue sky; and the water of San Diego Bay. Tiny sailboats and motorboats moved slowly on the deep blue water, and sun glinted on its surface. I could see the breeze on the water if I looked hard enough. It was funny— I was always running from one project to another, in one meeting and out of another. I never stopped to take in a real moment and enjoy my surroundings. I unhurriedly looked around the beautiful room, that view, and in that moment I had a shift. I experienced an overwhelming peace and an open heart where I could be kind. My eyes softened as I looked around. These were not bad guys; they were my colleagues. I let go of my judgment and was washed over with love.

It was my turn to present. I was still in an almost altered state as I stood up and slowly passed out my presentation binders. I had good news to share; it had been a great quarter.

The presentation binders were meticulously put together; they were encased in a navy blue binder that was the same shade as our company's logo. Embossed on the first page was our company's logo and on each right-hand corner was our logo, shaded, appearing almost 3-D. The feel of the binder was heavy and impressive. It looked like I'd hired a desktop publishing company that might have only used its best people. But the truth was, I'd done it at home on my laptop with a graphics software package, "Publishing for Dummies." It took me all of two late nights.

I had time because I had no life.

When I started my presentation, I was pleased that the projector worked flawlessly from my laptop. What was really impressive with my presentation was not the amazing view graphs and pie charts that rotated with radiating colors more vivid than Miramax, but the awesome ability to sync the information off my PowerPoint presentation. It was a killer. The only thing that could have distracted the mesmerized all-male audience was Vegas strippers. And even the strippers might not have had a chance, because I was on fire.

The discussion at hand was the quarter's forecasts, projections, and revenue. More specifically, the revenue margin and growth—basically, what kind of profits my department had brought in during the past three months. Sales were at an all-time high. We were selling at margins that were fat; the company had never seen net revenue soar so high. When you have good news, everyone wants to listen.

The success of my team came from the implementation of the business plan that I presented when I started my new position. I was drawing on basic and solid methodologies and ideas, but the company thought it was cutting-edge and too daring, so I got pushback from Eric, who wasn't big on critical assumption and strategic planning. I stood firm and made changes, like switching the sales reps' compensation to a wide-margin plan with a sliding scale. The results: Everyone made more money. But it was the tricky stuff, such as knowing the details of the market and the competition, that made us first of class in our field. My library of business journals, books, and magazines was paying off. I avoided making my own mistakes and benefited from their success, too.

Senior management, the big boys, were pleased with our expanding pipelines of opportunity. Everyone, especially these boys, would take home fat bonuses this quarter, and it would continue for the next year. My audience grinned when I showed them the under-budget figures and increased margin slide. But things got out of hand when I showed the over-projection slide—they were already swimming in the future swimming pools in their backyards.

When I was done, senior vice president Eric gave me a "Nice job, Ryley."

My high from the meeting lasted all of five minutes. That's how long it took to return to my desk, where the madness resumed. I was treading water because of the inadequacies of operations. My present definition of corporate America was "You share the pain inflicted by others, who cause the pain, but they don't feel it—they just watch us do all we can do to stop it."

I wanted something different. Not just a difference in the bottom line—a real difference. The majority of my waking hours were spent in that office; I wanted to be proud of something more than a paycheck. Maybe Sarah was right. I wanted my fingerprints on something terrific, like saving a baby from a burning building, something life-altering. But instead, I was burning out, losing passion.

I had been looking for the miracle book to give me instantaneous miracles. Instead, it was teaching the steps of embracing a process and letting go of fear, anxiety, and blaming, the mind chatter that could only be soothed with love and forgiveness. It was an arduous process.

I wasn't a very good student.

But there was something that finally sank in that day after what happened in the boardroom. A miracle is nothing more than a shift in perception. If we don't like what we are thinking, if it's causing us pain and we're ready to let go of that pain, a shift will occur. The shift was a part of a process—it wouldn't just happen—and it wasn't about denying what had happened or was happening that caused pain. It meant choosing not to dwell. Choosing love. It was like I couldn't blame my father for the thoughts I had. I had to take responsibility for making my life different. He couldn't hold me down anymore. I was doing that to myself.

Chapter Twenty-Four

"Let me not see myself as limited."

Coming home late from the office, with takeout in one hand, briefcase with laptop in the other, I was one step into the house when the phone rang. I grabbed the call just before the answering machine clicked on.

"Hello."

"Hey, Rye."

It was Toad.

"Hey, you!" I said.

"OK, I've started the job search in southern Cal."

"No way!" I dropped everything on the kitchen counter and began to strip off my pantyhose and suit until I was down to bra and panties. I headed toward the sweatpants in my bedroom closet with the cordless phone cradled in my shoulder nook, juggling suit and dinner, while Sarah filled me in.

"The best jobs are in LA, but there are two in San Diego that look good. When can I come out?"

"Right this very second."

"No, seriously. I'm trying to line up interviews in a week. I have a symposium in Orange County. Can I stay with you?"

"I'm hurt to think you'd even ask," I said, pulling on my sweatshirt. My head and the phone popped through the neck hole together.

"I'm ready, not just to leave Rochester because Rochester sucks, but also something else ...."

"Yeah?"

"I'm worried about you."

"Get out of here!"

"Seriously. You are working twenty-four hours a day; you're staying home. What's happened to you?"

"Oh, Toad," I said, opening up my takeout.

"You were my friend who used to have so much fun and used to laugh, always. And you haven't even been dating. What's going on?"

"Oh, God, Toad, I'm fine."

"Uh-huh," she said, more like a groan.

"Please."

"We'll see when I come out."

"Tell me about the interviews."

"I am really ready for a change. Everything is the same, and my job is going nowhere."

"So there is a God," I said, and I could feel her smiling back.

It would take a lot to move Toad to California all the way from New York. It would happen soon enough, when the layoffs came. Sarah would be saved, but the people who were let go were the core of what made her biotech company. Everything was drying up in Rochester, most Fortune 500's had already left, and Kodak was continuously downsizing. It was becoming a lifeless town, shriveled of all good opportunities. But not southern California. That's where biotech was happening, and Toad knew it. It would be a natural transition.

Having Toad come out wasn't the only good news. Back in the office the next day, everything seemed like business as usual, just another typical day.

Wrong.

Eric, my boss, the senior vice president, the guy with the eternal tan from golf, with a handicap that had gone from eighteen to seven this year, had been canned. That's right—fired. I was carrying in my usual artillery when I walked through the lobby: *Wall Street Journal, San Diego Business Journal* and *Business 2.0* under my armpit, briefcase with laptop, cell phone and CrackBerry, while balancing a cup of Starbucks. When my foot hit carpet coming off the marble lobby floor, I knew something was amiss. No one was working. Everyone was in full gossip mode without being incognito. The buzz around the office was louder than a swarm of killer bees. After two seconds in my office, I was granted the news from my secretary, the unofficial president and CEO of the rumor, tittle-tattle, idle-talk, chit-chat, and gossip channel.

God, I wanted his job more than anything. I mean, I *really* wanted his job more than anything!

I put my armload down as my mind raced to put things together. I thought about how my boss—I mean, ex-boss—had been out of the office lately more than his usual never-being-in-the-office self. Second, he'd been delegating more and more of his work to me since our revenue started going up. But more importantly, he'd asked me everything I knew about launching a start-up company.

I had been sucked into doing his additional and supplementary work. His time-consuming tasks became part of my regular work. I thought he gave me his work because he respected me, liked me, admired me. I should have figured something out when I even headed up one of his staff meetings because he never showed. When the meeting was over, I left the minutes and a page of notes on his chair behind his desk, like doing his homework and putting it in a place where the teacher wouldn't find out.

Once I sat down and checked e-mail, I saw the message from our president, Steve, that formally announced Eric's departure. It was soon followed up with a mini-conference call to the department heads, making his exit official. From internal phone lines to the water coolers, the office rippled with conspiracy theories.

I wondered if I could do his job.

Eric had been letting operations run the business. Come on, that department of namby-pambies should have been thinned out and replaced with fresh stock months ago. Eric never had a well-thought-out plan; he conducted business by the seat of his pants and led by fear tactics. How did the guy get the job to begin with? The obvious—master bull-shitter.

I tilted back in my chair and bobbed behind my desk, my brown alligator patent leather shoes resting on the corner of my desk. I sipped my latté, and slowly and methodically began to think.

Meetings scrolled through my head as wayward events started to fall in place. How did Steve not see what was going on? Well, he apparently had, because he fired the guy; I was the one who was clueless. People must have been pissed off about Eric's ivory-tower, dictator style of management, and they most likely had gone to Steve, which led to Eric's demise and dismissal. How could I not have seen this?

My mind raced on caffeine; my coffee went cold, but the flavor was still strong. It was too good to be true. Fired. There was no way I was going to get any real work done. I checked in with my direct reports to make sure that they weren't worried about their own job security or just plain flipping out. They were cool. I just couldn't get my mind off the idea that his job was now open; it was too intoxicating.

I called Toad.

"You're not going to believe it. My boss got canned."

"Really?"

"I want the job."

"But don't you think you're working too much as it is?"

I interrupted her. "There is no need for me to continue being a director when I've been doing vice-president work, or most of it. I mean, you know what I've been doing. OK, so maybe I'm fixated on the job for some of the wrong reasons, like the deluxe office and my unnatural obsession with the large amounts of money and power. But I have some good reasons for wanting his job, like making the company stronger and having the freedom to make decisions that would help the employees grow and prosper. I want to call the shots instead of doing senior management lackey work. The blood and sweat needed to make someone else look good is getting old."

"Rye, stop for a second and look at the big picture, like your quality of life—"

I interrupted her again. "ZerO is going to want the job. I'm sure there are countless others. The competition has to be in the front of my mind."

"Rye, you're getting a little nuts."

"No, I'm fine. I'm just brainstorming with you."

"Well, brainstorm this: Don't do it."

"Yeah, yeah, yeah. You're right. I'll just go and sign up for the nearest ass-breathing yoga class. What's it called?"

"You know, that might not be a bad idea." The sad thing was, she wasn't kidding.

"I gotta go."

"Call me back when you're home."

People were tense, walking around aimlessly, sharing in the gossip, worried about their own security. On the way to the bathroom I overhead "Serves him right … that tyrant." My secretary found out from his secretary that he had been escorted out the night before, late. Eric's secretary was queen for the day, dishing the scoop as if she'd just hit oil in her backyard.

He had no idea what hit him and didn't have a clue that everyone—and I mean everyone—was accusing him of really bad stuff. OK, so the guy wasn't the best senior manager— maybe he had been in over his head—but he wasn't a bad person. His body wasn't even cold yet, but he was being buried.

If Eric could have been a fly on the wall that morning, he'd have seen things that would have killed him. The people he trusted certainly didn't trust him. His "loyal" crew had bashed him from the first day he arrived. It's funny: As a manager, you never really know how people feel about you, whether they value you or not. It's because they fear for their own job security, and they may say and do things that aren't genuine. Sometimes you don't know how your direct reports really feel about you until it's too late, like, you're gone.

I actually began to feel sorry for him. Instead of looking at his faults, I reminded myself of his good. He made me a better manager and he gave me opportunities to grow. I stopped bashing him and extended my heart to him—a small shift.

Extending my heart to Eric didn't mean I didn't want his job. This would be my chance to put my ideas to work and bring the company out of the chaos that made my working days such a nightmare. I saw myself in his office, behind his massive desk. I fantasized about the money, more company stock, and his parking spot. Having your own parking spot was a sign that you'd made it. That sounded good. I could see my name in bold letters on the plaque outside his office.

Senior executive Jane Bond.

I began to strategize. Of course, there would be hard work, and not everything would be glorious. I'd have to campaign hard, make friends in the decision-making loop, get to know the board members. I'd have to bring the company out of the daily chaos that had been plaguing me. I could do it.

In concept, it sounded easy; in reality, I was a nervous wreck. What if they thought I was too young or under-experienced? Maybe I *was* too young and under-experienced. Would people take me seriously? There was no one my age at this level; maybe it had never been done. OK, maybe I could do the job, but getting it was a different matter.

I was desperate. Desperate times call for desperate measures. I read everything I could get my hands on, and then read some more. My favorite bookstore was downtown. As large as a supermarket, it offered newspapers in every language imaginable and aisle upon aisle of books in each department. The business department was like a candy store. I could easily spend a half-century in there.

I read everything on getting promoted, senior management strategies, how to get the job, and how to be a politician without being a politician and still understand corporate politics. You name it—I bought it and read it. I skimmed countless books until one day, I left the business department and wandered over to the self-help section. It was like moving from the right side of my brain to the left.

That's where I found a blue paperback with puffy clouds on the cover: *Dream Big—Let Yourself Get What You Want*. On the front and back covers were endless testimonials guaranteeing the effectiveness of the "Formula of Manifestation." It sounded too good to be real, but I'd try anything. Besides, Sarah would approve, and I'd just about exhausted the business section. At the beginning of the first chapter was an outline that explained the four money-back-guaranteed steps in obtaining your heart's desires.

Number one. Get into your gut; the book's exact words were "use your intuition and really 'Know What You Want.'" I had that one down.

Number two. Banish your fears. Uh-oh. That one seemed harder. The book described what it termed the "flinch factor." My flinch factor was that I thought I wasn't old enough, good enough, or deserving enough to get what I wanted. I skimmed to the chapter that encouraged the reader to acknowledge the fear and move through it.

Number three. See yourself living the dream. Use creative visualization to make your dream come true. The book advised staying with it even when the dream became out of focus—unlikely in my case. But number four, the key to all the others, had me stumped.

Number four. Completely release your heart's desires to God. Let it go; surrender. Let your mind relax and get to a place where you no longer are attached to the outcome of your dream. Detach from the result as you trust God to let it happen.

How could I possibly *not* be attached to the outcome? I'd heard Sarah talk about detachment, but this made no sense. Was I supposed to act like I couldn't care less if I got the job? Wasn't the outcome why I was working like a fiend and studying this book to begin with? I could see Sarah jumping up and down if I brought this title home, like all her work on me had paid off. I put it down, purchased another corporate promotions and strategy book, and headed for my car.

Driving home, I could not get those four steps out of my mind. I reached for a CD in my glove compartment to clear my head of these steps. My hand found the Bryan Ferry CD that Hank had given me. The car was hot. I pushed window buttons down to let in cool air. With both hands pushing against the steering wheel, I wrestled with the CD case. When it popped open too fast and the leaf that Hank gave me flew out the open window. "Oh, no!" I said aloud. Someone honked as I swerved to see where it went. Gone down the street. I tossed the CD to the back of the car and chose a Jack Johnson disc instead. I was still consumed with those four steps, especially the fourth.

Maybe releasing your heart's desire had something to do with faith, something I had little of. I murmured a meek prayer: "God, please show me that you exist and get me the job." I hoped God was on my side as I headed home.

Chapter Twenty-Five

"I can give up but what was never real."

Three weeks after Eric was out of my life, I had to let Sarah go back to Rochester. Her week of interviews and giving me hell about working too much had gone too fast. I realized I had hardly spent any time with her.

After dropping her off at the airport, I headed back to the office, and I found myself engulfed in the usual deluge of phone calls and meetings. And then, as I was looking for a contact name, I came across Pam's phone number.

I called her. "How come you never call anymore?"

"Hey, there … oh, you know, married life," she said in a Southern accent, kidding around. But then the old Pam shone through: "What's going on with your love life? Tell me about all those Californian hotties and those hard bodies. How's looking for Mr. Good Bod going?"

"Death Valley."

"What?"

"Drier than a boneless boner."

"Rye, these are your golden years of opportunity. You can't wait any longer. You'll get too old and all the good men will be going for the young bait. Get back out there."

"I'm not old. My career is just revving up."

"Rye, take it from the pro; don't waste any more time!"

"Hey, listen, gotta call you back. I'm on my way to a meeting."

"OK, but do." But she didn't mean it. With Pam married, our guy-ogling days were through, and she really didn't care about my career—or hers. She'd slipped into another world and had shed her single friends like an old skin. We'd stay in touch, maybe, but she wasn't holding her breath, waiting for me to call.

I didn't have a meeting, but I did want to take a moment. Talking to Pam made me feel sad; I'd gone through the old moves with none of the old feelings. I got up from my desk and headed for the ladies room. Walking through the office, as if nothing happened, I noticed ZerO had slipped into Steve's office and latched onto our president like a blood-sucking leech. What ZerO wanted was no secret. His head had found a new ass.

But then I overheard him bashing my department as I passed Steve's office. I shaped a gun with my index finger and thumb and pretended to shoot him over my shoulder as I passed the open door. Asshole. No one saw.

I feared the worst from ZerO.

I was back behind my desk, replying to e-mails, when in walked Rob Colter, one of my sales managers. He looked like he just had won the lottery.

"It's done!"

I looked at him, thinking, *And that would be ...?*

"We signed Bio-pro!"

He was referring to a 2.7 million-dollar deal.

"Way to go!" I said, standing up and giving him a football touchdown stance.

"That's not even the best."

I sat down, pretending to put an oxygen mask on my face.

He laughed. "We also have contracts on GI and Amge Technologies!"

"Get out of here! That puts you over quota for the year. Way to go, Rob! Outstanding!" I gave him a high-five.

"Ryley, make no bones about it. It's all about you."

"No, it's not!"

"I would never have had the team go after health care. You laid out the plan, and here we are. It worked, like you said it would. I love working for you!"

"Now, let's not get all mushy, Rob. You did it. You pushed your team forward and this is the result. Not bad."

We went through the deployment for the newly awarded business and discussed the critical support systems to make the new business stick. He left my office, still glowing, just as my phone began to ring.

Unfortunately, the warm glow from his good news turned into cow dung the moment I picked up. The death-sucking Dan, vice president of human resources, was on the other end, sounding for all the world like an obscene call from Dracula.

"So, Ryley, have you heard?" A slow inhale and a laborious exhale. Then another. Where was the disinfectant for my phone? "Looks like they picked our new boss," he said.

"Really?" I asked, trying to be cool, even though my heart stopped. Please let him be congratulating me.

"Outside consultant. Works for an outsourcing company." He chuckled and added, "What do they know about our company and how we operate?"

I wanted to agree with him but did the political thing. "Oh, Dan, I'm sure whatever decision the board and Steve made, it's the right one. They've been leading this company successfully for the past forty years."

I wanted to get off the phone, crawl under my desk, and

die. Wow. I was the one sucking for air—there was a numb, crushing feeling in the middle of my chest. My blood ran thick, like cement, blocking arteries to my heart, leaving me unresponsive.

Just as I dropped the phone into its cradle, Steve popped his head in. A distinguished man with silver hair in his late fifties or maybe early sixties, he was class with a capital C. His voice held the imprint of his schooling at Oxford. He looked like he should be modeling for Ralph Lauren, but of course, he'd never do that because it would be in poor taste. If I had a thing for older guys, he would be it, but I didn't, so he wasn't. Good thing; I'd already walked down that plank.

Steve had a warm smile and a quiet, reserved manner, but his steel-blue eyes gave him away. They were intense, revealing a powerful intelligence.

"Do you have a minute?"

I was dumbfounded; my head was still reeling from my conversation with Dracula, and I was afraid I wouldn't be able to remain professional. But I said the only thing I could say: "Sure."

Steve came in quietly, closed the door, and sat down in one of the chairs across from me. "I can imagine the rumor mill has started to turn. I thought I would come directly to you. I'm sure you have already heard something."

I wanted to hear it straight from his lips. Traitor! I had been loyal to him and given my best to the company and was hoping to have a chance to rise to the top.

"You know, I really haven't," I said. Thankfully, my voice sounded cool as a cucumber, revealing nothing.

"You know we're trying to fill Eric's slot. But more importantly, we're trying to position ourselves for a changing future. We think this is the time to take advantage of new movements in the marketplace." He paused and fixed me with those blue eyes. I nodded. "In order to add continuity to our competitive edge we, the board and I, think an outside perspective can help support our tactics. What do you think of a consultative approach?" he asked, with a slightly raised eyebrow.

"I think outsourcing is always a good idea; it's smart to draw on new ideas. External experts can bring a new frame of reference and a certain objectivity."

He smiled. "I knew you would agree, so you won't mind helping them out and getting them up to speed."

It was killing me, but I had to say it. "I'd be happy to. Anything I can do to assist or support."

He then opened up a manila folder that he had brought in with him. "OK, let's talk about this."

He unhurriedly opened the folder to reveal a single sheet of paper. He placed it in front of me and said, "What do you think?" as if he were playing chess and had just finished his move.

I looked at it; it was a huge salary and had added bonuses and stock; it was a small fortune.

"Steve, I think this is overly generous for a consultant."

"Hm?" His face was blank.

"Well, you're right. It would most likely be more than one person," I stammered.

"What?" He looked confused.

"But it's not clear how it would be allocated—"

"Ryley, this is *your* package; the consultants that are supporting you are hourly."

"What?" Blood rushed to my face.

"I came in to go over your package."

I couldn't believe what he was saying.

"I thought Dan had discussed this with you. I assumed

you understood that's why you have been acting VP. We need to go over the final offer," he said, with a ruffled look.

"Yes, of course." Without skipping a beat, the poker face came back. I continued, "Hm, well … this is generous but not quite what I had in mind for a complete package." Was that me talking? I felt as if I were far away, watching myself from another planet. My blood was speeding through my veins, and my heart was stuck in my larynx, my body in shock.

Looking over the paper, knowing it was actually meant for me was mind-blowing. I had no idea a VP got paid that much. The numbers were obscene—it was more than I could ever imagine. I played the game.

"You know, Steve, the revenue we've been hitting is a direct result of my efforts and strategy. I think it's fair to say that I'm the fresh perspective the company has needed. The past few years have been record-breaking, and though your offer is kind … well, it's not what I understand the market is providing for a position such as this."

I couldn't believe the words that dribbled out of my mouth. I was talking too much; I had no idea what the market was for positions like the one in front of me. I was paralyzed by my own perjury. The air was thick as cream cheese. I wanted to take it all back and give an embarrassing apology. Just as I was trying to figure out what to say and was about to open my mouth to do so, Steve interrupted. "Of course, Ryley, that's why we've offered you the position."

Pregnant pause. I had no idea what to say. I searched my mind for something sharp and impressive. I needed to backpedal. Nothing. I stared at him, like an actor on stage who has forgotten his lines.

He continued for me. "I've asked the board to put their best foot forward. I won't be able to change the salary."

Another pause; I was still blank.

Steve cleared his throat and smoothed his hair on the left side. "But we may be able to look at the stock."

Had I died and gone to heaven? He thought my lack of ability to verbalize was an on-purpose silence, a tactic. And he fell for it. God, I hoped he didn't think I was taking advantage of him. I didn't want him to think I was only in it for the money. But part of me was thrilled by the way this was going. I had the job.

"You know, Steve, I am willing to share the risk. Let's pony up on the bonus part. Let's put a direct percentage based upon net sales," I said, as if I were giving him a great break. But inside I was smiling.

He quickly jumped in. "Oh, I'm sure that could be possible." He tried to sound cool and his usual collected self, but his smile gave it away, like he had won the negotiations.

What Steve didn't know was that by the end of the third quarter, the company would be over the entire year's projections. He didn't know what Rob had just told me. With the recent contracts we had won and were in the process of closing, pipelines of opportunities were bursting, and revenue would be at an all-time high. He wasn't aware of my lowball projections. If the company hit just the year's projections, the bonus portion would be twice the original offer. I had scored in a big way.

We both won, actually. His bonus would be bigger too.

As Steve was leaving my office, he turned to face me. "Now that you're officially my right-hand person, I'm expecting you to work much harder to show the board what I know. You are a vice president now, Ryley. I'm looking forward to the results."

"You have my word."

Whip the thoroughbreds. Steve's philosophy and methodology—disproportionately pay your top performers as you disproportionately prod and push them. He believed the best would adapt. And I was the best.

Later that afternoon, my contract came down in a brown envelope marked "Confidential." I sent it over to my attorney for final blessings and signed it early the next morning.

I started to believe in miracles.

Chapter Twenty-Six

"Peace to my mind. Let all my thoughts be still."

Money never comes easily.

Even though we were hitting the sales numbers I expected, my new staff was a thorny bunch. If they'd lost their passion for the job before, they now had a new excuse for underperforming. The current rant of choice: "How can I do my job with so much upheaval?" What they really were saying but never would was, "I can't take responsibility for my actions if the company won't do everything for me." The only way I could motivate these slouches was to be tough and unbreakable.

I was definitely not feeling like someone who was seeking her spiritual truth—there was no peace in prodding people by any means necessary. There were times I had to encourage these select few by fear. I didn't feel any genuine connection or loving compassion as I let them wonder about their future. I felt evil.

My goal, when I started the new position, was to build synergy and redefine process flow. We all knew that the company was operations-driven and not sales-driven; this flaw needed immediate correction, but it had to be done carefully. ZerO gave me major pushback and was excruciatingly bitter because I was in the job that he wanted. I didn't blame him; if the tables were turned, I wouldn't have been thrilled, either.

"Ryley, you just haven't been in the business that long. With no ill respect, I don't think you understand how we do business here. You can't understand operations with your background."

I smiled. "Thank you, Stan, for that vote of confidence. However, let's get to the business at hand." My voice was calm and slow. "Stan, let's look at refocusing and redefining our—"

"Let's not muddy the waters with operations, Ryley. You don't understand how we do things, and you don't want to trouble your pretty little head. Let the other departments try these new little tactics of yours," he said, with a perverted little wink.

"Stan—"

"Ryley, you don't get it. Operations is fine; it's the other departments that are not working."

His stubborn, monotonous tune was exhausting. After one of our talks I was invariably furious and filled with doubts. Was I in over my head? I felt like I was treading water with weights tied to my ankles, with vultures circling above, piranhas below. There was no one to turn to for advice.

So after a long day of combat, I went back to my favorite bookstore and read everything I could get my fingers on about changing management, how to overcome conflict in the workforce, building successful teams. I also scoured the Internet for cutting-edge theories from business journals and newspapers. I checked business development Web sites, anything that could shed insight on my dilemma. The good news was that I wasn't the only senior manager with this problem.

Those late nights I still found myself thinking of Hank, wondering what he was doing. He was someone I could imagine talking to about my concerns at work. Did he think of me at all? I hoped he'd give me one of his notorious out-of-the-blue calls. Nope. There was nothing. Only space. Work space.

So one evening, on the way out of the office, I picked up the phone and called him. The phone rang three times before he answered. I hung up immediately. His voice was the same: unchanged, calm, and smooth. His "hello" replayed over and over in my head.

The only thing that would get that voice out of my head was therapy from Toad. So like most nights when I was beyond stuck, I called her.

"Hello?"

"Hey, Toad."

"What's taken you so long to call back? I've been calling you nonstop on your cell and home."

"Oh, I'm still in the office."

"God, it's almost ten o'clock your time."

"Yeah, I know …."

"OK, OK. I got two offers—one in LA and one in San Diego. We have to talk."

"Which one's better?"

"Probably LA. But they really want me in San Diego. I could probably get the same, if not more, pay in San Diego, but it's a smaller company."

"What's better long term?"

"Probably LA. What do I do?"

We spent the next hour going over the pros and cons on both. She was really torn. I wanted her to come to San Diego more than anything, but I knew she'd have to make her own decision. I needed to stay neutral.

I slowly said, "OK, here is something original. I'm going to say something that you always say to me. You have all the right answers inside of you to make the perfect choice for you. You have to get quiet and listen for the answer."

"My God, you're right! I need to meditate on this. Why didn't I think of it?'

"You did."

She took a deep breath, as if she already felt better. "Thanks. How's the new job?"

"Terrible."

"What's going on?"

"It's a bloodbath, and my blood is all over." I gave her the detailed update and instead of being bored by it all, she had the solution that I'd been thinking of myself but hadn't come to terms with yet.

"You have to reorganize. The only way to have a winning team is to have a winning team. Change your staff and things will change. Can Stan and the other moron, and you'll be a lot happier."

"Yeah, but how do I convince my boss? I haven't been in the position that long to just slash and burn."

"You have all the answers within you. Just get quiet so you can hear them, meditate, or, in your case, try going for a run."

"Figures. When I really need your opinion, you clam up."

The truth was that she was right; she was always so damn right. If I was to be taken seriously, I had to make changes that would send a message of the strength of my leadership.

The next day the sun shone weakly through my office window, barely casting a shadow on the floor in front of my desk. No music—just the clack of the keyboard as I prepared a detailed business proposal outlining my plans for realigning my staff. The rare overcast sky created a somber mood, making my movements slow down as I worked meticulously on my critical assumptions. Then I checked my work, filled gaps, and added support to make a stronger case.

Finally satisfied, I typed an e-mail to Steve asking for a meeting the following week. I attached the proposal, took a deep breath, and clicked "send."

The day of our meeting, I was more nervous than I'd thought possible. As I walked to Steve's office, my pantyhose stuck to the inside of my legs. Sweat in the middle of my back made my shirt feel like a large piece of tape. From the outside, I looked collected; inside, I was a shaky mess.

I wanted to joke with his secretary—"Is the chap here? Could you tell the chap I'm in?"—but knew my delivery would be off. She'd probably walk in before me to whisper, "Look out ..."

I knew he wouldn't agree to staff changes so early in my new position. He likely had scripted a brilliant and unshakable case on how he'd made the wrong decision to hire me and pay me so handsomely.

His secretary announced my arrival, and I slipped through the door. I sat down in the chair across from him, his sleek desk defining the gap between us. I began to start my well-rehearsed speech. He quickly interrupted me, looking straight in my eyes. "Ryley, I reviewed your plan." He cleared his throat, reaching for a sip of water. Here it was: He was gonna fire me. He continued. "You don't need my permission to go ahead with it. Remember, I trust you." I was dumbfounded, completely unprepared for this reaction. I sat there like a limp stalk of celery that has been in the refrigerator too long. Speechless. OK, so I got that wrong.

He moved right on, changing the subject, and mentioned

that he'd been thinking about acquiring a small company. It was a good idea. I knew the company well, so I told him what I knew and that I thought it was a good idea.

We talked no more than thirty minutes and then I was out the door. If the meeting had had a title, it would be something like "Surmountable—there aren't any rules."

On the way out, I was thinking too hard about what he had said about trusting me, thinking about the changes I'd make, thinking too hard, I guess, because I lost track of my body. I tripped, falling forward, arms flailing to catch my balance, and my nose made solid contact with the wall by his door. The result was a bruise that I would have to explain the next day. I tried to brush it off as I pulled down on my blazer.

Steve looked at me without missing a beat. "You're running the day-to-day business like it should be run. Just be careful of what you walk into." His steel-blue eyes went soft and warm. I smiled back, my ears burning with embarrassment.

Steve's intention was to go to Wall Street and do all the things needed to propel our company forward. An IPO was the next step. As we got to know one another better. I relaxed, stayed clear of his wall, and in no time we were a working team.

The organization did change. When I called ZerO into my office to let him go, he didn't make things easy. He started off by assuming the best defense was a good defense.

"You've been sent to terminate with prejudice."

"Excuse me?"

"Age discrimination."

He was like a wild horse. He sensed I was afraid, and he lit into me and wouldn't be taken. Stan was one of those conservatives who never learned to break-dance or get a tattoo or even understand those who did. I steeled myself for a fight. But then something strange happened. Instead of calling in human resources to finalize the exit, I took a breath. I mean, I took a real breath—slow and steady. And in that breath, I slowed down and began to see him differently. He was getting fired, for God's sake. He wasn't attacking me. He was scared, and behind that angry, mean face was a call for help.

His fearful eyes said it all, so I let him go with dignity, and let him say all that he had to say. I finalized it with "Stan, you are better than this place, and you will survive."

Seven weeks later, I had my two new hires, and the senior staff was complete. Things began to fall into place, but the long hours continued. My world narrowed until all I lived, breathed, or thought about was work. I was wrapped around my job, like a bad egg roll. I was losing myself—chaos in my head with no harmony on the playing field, no relief in sight.

In the midst of this insanity, help came, not in the form of a knight in shining armor, but a five-foot-two bundle of wisdom and love. Toad called. She had taken the job in San Diego. We whooped, yipped and discussed the where and when, and finally, when we hung up, I thanked the gods who brought her to me. Then I stopped to wonder when we'd see each other—I had so much to do at work.

Sarah moved in with me a few weeks later. It wasn't a permanent arrangement but I wanted so much to have her around. Staying with me would give her a chance to start her job and get to know the city before she picked out a place of her own. It was great having her with me, but I hadn't counted on her being so pushy. Long distance, it was easy to ignore her advice. But having her in my house was another matter. She tried everything to get me to take meditation classes, until one day, it was so bad. Don't ask me how I gave in to the other side. The truth was, I was so stressed out that I hoped she knew something I didn't.

The bags under my eyes wilted down my face from lack of sleep. I micro-analyzed every meeting and scenario at the office, making myself wacky. I was waking up at three in the morning with brilliant insight that would keep me up for the rest of the night. Other nights, I collapsed into bed immediately after getting home, not even bothering to brush my teeth, out cold until morning.

I started to gain weight, a pound here and a pound there, until I couldn't zip or button my pants; even my underwear was tight. When my skirts wouldn't zip all the way, I closed them with a safety pin hidden under my blazers. The scales said I had only gained eight pounds; it felt more like fifty.

Sarah made me wear sweats so I'd be comfortable, and she warned me that when we were in class she wouldn't talk to me. She wanted to be sure I wouldn't lose "the essence of what meditation is all about—quiet." I looked over my shoulder when I walked into the class, afraid I would be recognized—not that I knew anyone other than Toad who actually meditated. I was completely taken by surprise and could not believe that I actually liked the classes.

Maybe it was the overstuffed soft pillows in an Indian damask that were casually placed on the floor, or the scent of incense drifting in the air. Most likely, it was because it was so different from work. The class melted away the hardness of my day. What was undeniable was the magic of a mind at peace.

The first class didn't transform me; it was around the third or fourth that I saw the changes. For me, it was all about the breathing—I mean, really breathing; not just the in/out motions but the ability to slow down and feel my breath, feel the oxygen fill my lungs, and imagine that oxygen reaching my blood. I needed to hear air come through my nostrils and make its way all the way down, all the way down to the depths of my soul. The knots in the upper-back muscles, wedged underneath my shoulder blades, started to dissolve the more I meditated.

I craved the silence and stillness. As I learned to relax and still my chattering mind, my thoughts began to become clear. Instead of just making it through the day and repeating hour upon hour in the office, buried under papers and chained to my phone, I began to make a conscious priority to journey into the light within myself. Some days it worked; most days it didn't.

But on the days it did work, it felt like I was mothering myself and listening to my greatest and deepest needs. During class, I discovered that by simply changing my mantra during meditation, I could change the depth of my healing. I might say over and over, "I am at peace, I am at peace, I am at peace," or on another day, "I am filled with gratitude and thankfulness, I am filled with gratitude and thankfulness," or maybe, "Only good lies before me, only good lies before me," or "All is well—I am safe, all is well— I am safe, all is well—I am safe."

I was learning to care for myself, to seek that calm center. After a hard day at work, I'd fill the bathtub with soothing hot water scented with lavender oil, illuminate the room with candles, and sink into that warm relaxation. I would close my eyes to find the stillness once again, and if I couldn't find it, I would create affirmation mantras to find that still place within. The more I found the stillness, the easier it was to get there.

It wasn't just meditation that was making me feel better. After our meditation class, sometimes in the car or on the back patio when we got home, Sarah would take out *A*

Course in Miracles and choose an exercise or just read. It was on one of those days that my life shifted again.

"Oh, here, Ryley, I love this: *Beyond the body, beyond the sun and stars, past everything you see and yet somehow familiar, is an arc of golden light that stretches as you look into a great and shining circle. And all the circle fills with light before your eyes. The edges of the circle disappear, and what is in it is no longer contained at all. The light expands and covers everything, extending to infinity, forever shining and with no break or limit anywhere. Within it, everything is joined in perfect continuity. Nor is it possible to imagine that anything could be outside, for there is nowhere that this light is not.*"

She closed the book slowly, smiled, and walked away.

And there it was, right at my fingertips yet beyond my grasp. I could see it distinctly but could barely make it out. It was only a picture in my mind, a fleeting thought that whirled and pirouetted before my mind's eye. A memory of who I really was and what I was made of, a piece of God, a piece of good. It only lasted for a second and then it was gone.

Chapter Twenty-Seven

"Love is the way I walk in gratitude."

When Sarah moved in, she really moved in, and I didn't know if I was ready for it. She became my social coordinator and the master of my social calendar. Well, actually, she was my social calendar. Before Sarah, there was just work. Now, there was work and Sarah. I didn't know who I was married to anymore. I'd become a bigamist.

"OK, I got the whole weekend planned for us."

"You know, I might have some plans."

"This is California. They don't like it when you work all the time here. Have you forgotten you live in paradise now?"

"Huh, ha-ha." I faked a laugh for her benefit. "Well, actually, I might have plans that don't include work."

"Uh-huh," she said, completely ignoring what I'd said. "Go for a run, clear your head, and then I'll go over our plans."

She had been living with me for close to three months; it was beginning to feel like three million years. It was bad enough that she got me into meditation and I was kinda liking it. Next, she would be taking away my coffee and handing me carrot juice in the morning, or turning my living room into a Buddhist temple. Don't get me wrong—she was making my life better. I just wished she'd do it somewhere else. And another thing, her intuition was in overdrive.

"Don't worry. Don't worry. Have you forgotten my house

is in escrow? I'll be out of here in less than thirty days … and you're really gonna miss me then."

Doubt it, I thought, as I gave her a fake "Oh, yeah, sure" smile.

It was Saturday. Finally. Time to sleep and forget about the past week. A day to water the plants in my tiny garden and watch the water sparkle and dance on each leaf. Or maybe go browsing in a good bookstore and walk slowly, enjoying the full moment by myself and pretending Sarah didn't live with me. I grabbed the morning papers and leather journal under one arm, mail and key in the other, and headed to a large Starbucks for some space.

Once I was through the papers, I opened my leather-bound journal and began to list all the vast and wonderful things I was grateful for. A sunbeam found my hand and left a bright strip of light on my right knuckles. I stopped writing, looked at the magnificent light, and found peace. I had found stillness and a quiet mind that didn't rattle and chatter. I had written five pages and was on item 167 when I realized I had arrived. I was thankful. It had taken a long time, but my life was feeling whole. I looked around, slowly taking in my surroundings, and it was as if I was connected to everyone in the room, not different but the same. I was one with my surroundings. No, I wasn't high on caffeine. Was it the affirmations that had made their way to my living thoughts and changed the way I looked at and felt about things? Sarah's hard work on me had paid off; I began to understand what she meant about finding my authentic self.

I'd like to say that I woke up and all of a sudden there was peace of mind and miracles in my life, but the truth is, it was a process.

I could feel my breath again—or maybe for the first time. I sat there in that chair in the corner and closed my eyes and listened to my breath, and it sounded good and strong.

I found my way to serenity, and it felt good. My surroundings seemed clearer, sharper, more distinct. Was it because
more oxygen was making it to my brain from all the meditation, or was it because I was slowing down and enjoying
what was around me and living fully in the moment?

My cloudless vision wasn't the only thing that was
changing in my life. Simplicity. I began to simplify my work—
delegate more and stop overanalyzing everything I did. My
urges to find new tasks at work were also disappearing; I
felt as if what I was doing was all that was needed. It spilled
over into my personal life. Less is more. I cleaned out closets,
partly to make room for Sarah but also to get rid of the
clutter. The biggest change was my car. The mobile home,
with every accessory of life, was converted to a car—clean
and streamlined for transportation.

After a morning with no plans and plenty of breathing
room, I continued to write in my journal until I could write
no more. I finished my second cup of java and went to the
gym. When I arrived home, there was Sarah, like a puppy
waiting for her owner.

"Maybe *you* need to get out," I suggested.

"I did, Rye. I'm back. Now, let's go play!"

"Let me shower first. What did you have in mind?"

"There is this great area where local artists sell their
stuff—Cedros … something."

"OK, but we have that invite thing from work tonight."

"I think I want to stay in tonight," she said sheepishly,
trying to sound like the old me.

I ignored her response. "Hey, I told you about it weeks
ago. C'mon, it's the only thing I've had on my calendar for
months. A group of us are going out for drinks and dinner
tonight—it'll be fun."

"Nah. I was looking forward to a quiet evening at home,"

she said, pulling two bottled waters from the fridge and putting them in her bag.

"Come on. You said yes a week ago ... and there is someone I want you to meet."

"Changed my mind." Then she took a minute to ask, "Who?"

"A doctor ... who sails and is into yoga ..."

"Nah."

"Come on. Stay out of your PJ's and come out. We'll leave at seven."

She stammered, "You know, I—"

"Stop. I know what you're thinking. I know what's going through your head, but it doesn't have to be that way with men. It's like all the stuff you teach me; you change your mind about something and you shift and a miracle comes shining through. Come on. It will be fun!"

I said nothing more and headed for the shower. She sulked on the coach.

"I really don't want to go out!" she screamed up the stairs. Unfortunately, she had no choice. I'd threatened to bring them over if she didn't come with me. Sarah knew me well enough to know I meant it too. She gave in.

Sarah was acting weirder than usual. It was six-thirty, and she was racing around, spinning like a girl in her hula hoop. I gave her a glass of wine and told her to calm down. It was partly my fault. I had her trying on twelve outfits that she hated, and finally, she ended up with something comfortable— her favorite khaki blazer (that might as well have been a lab coat from work), white mock turtleneck, khakis, and flats.

"You're not wearing that!" I screamed.

"What's wrong with this?"

"It doesn't show off your great body, and you look like you're still at work! How about that cute pink skirt?"

"OK, I'm not going." She was pissed and had had enough.

"OK, OK. Let's go. We're running late." The weather had been exceptionally warm all week, and I warned her that she would be hot. I didn't dare push harder to get her to change. I, on the other hand, wore a cool yellow-and-white summer dress and the cutest sandals. Before we walked out the door, Sarah ran up to put on lots of gold accessories and two coats of makeup. She looked like Liberace, in drag, in a lab coat.

Climbing into the car she asked, "Where are we going?"

"The yacht club," I said, as she reapplied lipstick on her already-red lips.

"You know, I changed my mind again. Let's go back, please." And there it was: sheer panic in her eyes.

I looked square into her face and said, "I promise you, it will be OK, and I promise you, you'll have fun. These are really good people. You'll see."

She said nothing, stiff as a board. Ten minutes later, she said, "OK, tell me about the guy."

"He's a doctor in oncology at Scripps Hospital. He's lived out in California since he was a kid. His brother, who's an attorney, works with me and is a super guy. He helped me on the close of my house. Oh, did I say he's a lead doctor at this alternate medical clinic? Yepper, he's really into yoga! Wink, wink," I said playfully.

"What? Why haven't you mentioned him?" she said sarcastically, playing back for the moment.

"I didn't want you to go weird on me, like ask a million questions when I was just feeling out the situation for you."

"Why do you hold back information? If you don't tell me, it hurts. Your joy is mine. Stop doing that!" she said, but her kidding around turned pissed because I was making her do something that she didn't want to.

She brushed me off and continued, "Well, if he's into yoga, it can't be that bad."

"Yeah, yeah." I was egging her to go on.

She went back to quiet and scared. I knew all about this guy from a lunch meeting that I had with our legal team, weeks ago. His brother tried to set him up with me but he sounded more like Sarah's type.

His name was Robert Rockefeller and no, he wasn't related. He was Sarah's perfect match, actually: a brainiac metaphysical who loved to sail. He even sounded physically perfect for her—dark and lean. And for the first time in the years that I had known Sarah, she was trying to be open—in her rigid, scared, and obstinate kind of way. Open to the possibility of loving a man. Well, kinda.

"You're going to love it at the yacht club. It's very you!" I said, trying to cheer her up.

"When were you … uh … what do you mean, it's very me?"

"It's a sailing haven. You'll see—it's very East Coast, swank, prep. You'll fit right in."

When we arrived, the yacht club was beautiful—something right out of *Town and Country*—a New England-style clubhouse, weathered gray shingles, and classic white trim. It had the feel of money even before we stepped into the lobby. The grounds were meticulously manicured, not a blade or leaf out of place, tennis courts to the left, the San Diego Bay to the right and behind the building. The parking lot was filled with endless Mercedes, Jaguars, BMWs, and even two Rollses, minus chauffeurs. Best of all were the boats. I had never seen so many yachts and mega-yachts—luxurious masterpieces tied neatly to their slips.

The sound of seagulls and twanging boat halyards blew in on the light breeze that was coming off the water, filling my lungs with the salty ocean air. The water sparkled and dazzled my eyes, as golden light flecks spun from the rippling water. A blue heron soared above, its call reminding me of Maine.

The front lobby was grand and austere, making me feel a bit out of place. We walked into the clubhouse bar, passing the polished sailing trophies that glittered in handsome mahogany cases. The glossy, hardwood floors had inlaid designs made from African hardwoods. Nautical brass fittings gave the place an aura of refinement.

As we walked into the lounge, I stepped back to admire the prominent teak bar, shining under numerous coats of varnish. Sailing flags, half models, and burgees were everywhere, making the room look just like a yacht-club bar should. Sarah relaxed; her passion for sailing was getting the better of her.

Gathered around each cocktail table, well-groomed club members relaxed in overstuffed, worn leather chairs. I headed to a large table of ten people; I recognized most of them from work. I sat Sarah down right next to Robert, and she shot me a look that all about said, "Don't you fucking leave me here." Her face said abandonment. Abandoned by strangers, like a baby eaten by dingoes.

I didn't want to, but was forced to sit between two strangers at the other end of the table from Toad, the only other seat available. The two men that I was wedged between were not from my company and were both dressed in casual sailing attire. She gave me the look of "I am going to kill you," but I was uncomfortable too. I had no idea who the guys next to me were.

Toad was too far away. It felt like miles to something familiar—maybe this *was* a bad idea. Once she started talking to Robert, she relaxed, and she looked like she was OK and actually having fun. But now I wasn't. Robert's pals immediately started joking around, making me feel clumsy and awkward.

"So, Ryley," a stranger at the end of the table said. "Looks like we're set for the game."

I had no idea what he was talking about, so I smiled and gave him a cool, "You bet." I looked up at the two televisions in opposite corners of the room and saw a basketball game was on.

"So what do you think?" he continued.

I had no idea what the score was and couldn't stand all those eyes staring at me like I was supposed to give some type of vapor-genius sports-announcer answer. I smiled and signaled the waitress for a drink. The twenty-one questions continued, and somehow I threw out the answers that they were looking for. Thank God for the sports section that morning; at least I knew that the Bulls were playing. Inside, my stomach was a mass of enzymes, gnawing away. I felt out of sync and wanted to get out of there—fast. The guys at the table knew each other and almost spoke in their own code.

Then, suddenly, a guy to my immediate right quietly and smoothly leaned over and gently whispered in my ear, "Don't worry; they're not as bad as they seem. They're actually good guys. You're doing fine, and your friend looks like she's beginning to feel comfortable. She'll be okay."

My cheeks flushed. Who was this guy who could read minds, or had I looked that uncomfortable? I stared dumbfounded at him. He made me feel instantaneously relaxed and connected to him. Was he extraordinarily perceptive or just clairvoyant? With a few words he had cut to the heart of my concern and helped me to relax. I felt a strong connection to him, as if I had known him from somewhere before. He went back to interacting with the group, as I was frozen numb and still staring at him.

I slowly and carefully looked around the room to see if anyone else saw what I saw. Did anyone else notice he was clairvoyant too? Was he reading others' thoughts this very minute or just mine?

I looked at him; I mean, I *really* looked at him. He had an all-American kind of face, and the light above his blonde hair gave off a glow like a halo. He wore a nautical sweater and sailing shorts. The lights were too low to figure out what color his eyes were; my guess was blue. His body type, medium. His hands were wrinkled by the sun and hard work from being on boats too much. He had the most unusual flat fingernail beds.

His nature was calm and quiet, not the aloof type but more of the polite and distinguished type—friendly and approachable. It was his gentleness that gave him a sexual and sensual aura. This easy manner made conversation flow without effort. When I began talking, I found out that he was from the East Coast too; he had lived in California since college, more than ten years. It was these years that added to his laid-back coolness.

After a while, I went for the jugular. I asked him what type of music he liked, and instead of the safe "everything" answer, he casually said, "I started out a rock fan, and then the college music original tunes—you know, the gritty renditions of classics. Stuff you could dance to or bang your head to. New wave, a little funk, and then finally made my way to the rapture of jazz. Wynton Marsalis. I'm a big Ray Charles fan. No country or acid rock."

Good taste. What can you say when lightning strikes? Nothing.

I began to stammer. He sensed my tongue growing fat and offered to get me another drink. The conversation and the drinks flowed like the Colorado River. And was I falling.

I had a beer sandwich for dinner. And the popcorn appetizer was not going to cut it. I was drunk.

He tried to make conversation. "I like living here. Southern California can feel like a vacation."

"Really. What do you do?" And there it was. The question I hated, but I really wanted to know and after a few drinks I just blurted it out.

"Oh, I work on boats."

Oh, dear God, I thought. *I have nothing in common with this guy. He probably only makes enough to scrape by.*

He was polite enough not to ask what I did. Thank God.

But there was something about this guy, something different. I watched him interact with the group—the guy was not only well liked but deeply respected. He was funny, too. Nothing original made its way out of my mouth. There was no use in talking; I'd screw it up. So I asked him open-ended questions and listened. I asked him everything he'd done on the planet before I met him. Seeing that he was the perfect gentlemen, he complied. I felt as if I had missed him for centuries, and now my soul was finally at peace. I wondered if he felt the same.

"I've never met anyone like you, Ryley." They say when lightning strikes, it only strikes once; if that's the case, I was struck down and burning in flames. I was trying not to buy into the love-at-first-sight stuff, but this strange man made me so peaceful.

I signaled across the table to Sarah. We met in the bathroom. I wanted to reveal my discovery and see how she was holding up. Sarah was more than eager to listen. "So what's happening on your side of the table? Who is that guy?" she asked, before heading for a stall.

"Me? What about you?" I asked, standing there staring at her back as she shut the door.

"I'll fill you in, but I have scoop on yours."

"What? How is that possible?"

Sarah was washing her hands and drying them off when she turned into a newspaper reporter. "Well, his name is Gordon Whitney. He's into boats. Went undergrad at Carnegie Mellon, started grad work at UCSD, ended up in the boating business but switched into technology of boats—makes a good living. Excellent sailor. Has a younger brother."

"Jesus, how do you know all this stuff? What about your guy?"

"Oh, it's fine, but I had to get the goods for you."

"Jesus ... can you fucking relax and have a good time?"

"OK, OK ... I like this guy. I'd see him again!"

"No way!" I said, with a touchdown motion.

"You gotta stop doing that. It is so lame."

"Shut up," I said. "Give it up—details."

"I like him," she said casually. "But come on. I just met the guy."

"Yeah, yeah, yeah." Knowing she wouldn't give me any more and getting bored with her aloofness, I said, "Do you think I make more money than my guy?"

"Rye, you make more money than everyone. Come on. We're going down to his boat for cocktails."

"He has a boat?"

Back at the table and right after we downed our last drink, Gordon stepped up to pull out my chair and take us to his boat. And that's when it was all over. He was so short that he might as well have come up to my belly button. OK, I'm exaggerating. He was my height, maybe one inch taller. Five-foot-nine or nine and a half. In most people's books, that isn't a midget, but when you only date guys that tower over you, it is.

I was bummed but still committed to having fun.

It was a forty-two foot Herreshoff wooden sailboat, built in 1928. The boat was a flawless vessel that had been restored to its natural beauty. The classic lines gave it form and function that were expressed in a pure language. Timeless style. Just like Gordon. The details made it so extraordinary—the exposed wood was spray-varnished rather than brushed, making a perfect, glasslike sheen. The inside was like a small suite at the Four Seasons, with everything in its place. It was beautiful.

The waves gently rocked the floating poem in its slip, as eight of us sipped cocktails from the teak and rosewood bar. I sank softly in the leather settee in the main salon and let out a slow, "Ah-h-h."

Gordon sat beside me. "So do you always have this effect on men when they first meet you?" I blushed; he brought me back to heaven.

When the evening ended, he drove me home, walked me to the door, and placed a slip of paper into the palm of my hand. It was his phone number. He whispered to call as he gently smudged my forehead with his thumb.

I called him a half hour later. "Oh, hello," he said with a straight tone, yet kidding around. "You are not going to believe this—on my way home, I ended up surfing. My clothes are all wet. Don't ask me how my car got in the ocean. I guess I was thinking about you."

I laughed and said, "I know what you mean. That's why I called."

We talked until the sun rose, a date that never stopped.

If I was entitled to miracles, one had just landed right in my arms.

Chapter Twenty-Eight

*"Steady our feet, our Father. Let our doubts be quiet
and our holy minds be still, and speak to us.
We have no words to give to You. We would but listen …
God is but Love, and therefore so am I …
It is Here that we find rest."*

Time stood still, as it does when you are in love. From the first moment, we both knew. We knew this was different. We had found each other; the search was over. He wasn't my knight in shining armor—he was better. He was someone who got me and could unconditionally accept. We could wonder in the discovery of each other and realize that we didn't have to be perfect and that would be OK. It would be enough.

There wasn't a person who didn't think I was nuts. The responses were the same: "Slow down." Sarah was my biggest critic.

"Don't you think you're going a little too fast?"

"You're the one who sees Robert all the time. I thought you'd approve."

"I do, I do. It's just a little early to be naming your kids."

"Give me a break. Listen, there are no secrets between Gordon and me, no hidden treasures, no bad baggage. He didn't come from a family of criminals. He's not having an affair with anyone. I don't work with him. It's different now. I found myself first before he found me."

She was in preacher mode. "Yeah, yeah, I know all that, but come on. You're talking about marriage and you've been dating three months."

"It's not like we are setting a date, but come on. Pam's right; the clock is ticking and I don't want mine stuck. I don't want to be one of those women who waits until she's forty and has to take infertility drugs."

"Oh, please."

I had pushed a button. Sarah knew all about infertility drugs; it was one of the products at her new company. She knew the despair her forty-something women had to endure and the percentages of cysts and tumors women got from too many treatments. I wanted no part of her research; my eggs were good and strong and not in tiny wheelchairs yet.

I continued my argument. "No, I'm serious. I've done all I want to do alone. I've got to travel all over with work—great hotels, gotten everything out of my system that I thought meant something to me—but more importantly, I realize I can support myself, love myself, even my body." I took in a deep breath. "Here's the thing: I don't need to marry my dad or a guy that is a postcard image of a Marlboro man. I don't need a man to accept myself."

Her arms were crossed tightly over her chest. She didn't like what I was saying but was willing to let me speak.

"This is what I am learning, Toad: It's OK to open my heart and let people in, even if they don't agree with my values. I understand that I'm not perfect. It's all OK; it's actually good. When I give them the room to 'get' me, to take time to know me, they do, because we all are really the same at the core." Toad's arms softened; she wanted to interrupt but I didn't let her. "I'm far from perfect, but I'm learning that it's OK to share my struggles and mistakes and not be a control freak like my dad but just relax and just be. Listen, Gordon makes me laugh, and he understands me. He gives me space, acceptance, and support. What else is there? This means something to me. Can't you be supportive?"

She finally shut up and gave up. For the moment.

OK, I wasn't stupid. I still had to see if our relationship had legs. Could it support a roaring fight or hard times? Could it still stand after he had the flu? Could I see myself in his family?

Sure, everything was great—it was the beginning. Our moments were living in the now to the fullest. Gordon loved to hold hands and touch in public, like movie theaters and at dinner or just crossing the street. His hand would soon find mine, as my palm would perfectly rest in his. I was still a little self-conscious about his height and replaced my heels with flats.

But on the couch, we were on a level playing field, and I could relax and see him for him and not his height. I loved the way he smudged my forehead when we were on the sofa watching TV, like he was making sure I was real and not going to float away.

Gordon was the type that, if he did cook, outside of his one and only meal, he would try to cook something at 700 degrees for fifteen minutes instead of at 350 for thirty minutes. OK, so he wasn't a cook, but he gave me a different way to accept things.

I began to slow down—slow down my breathing and slow down my living and enjoy my life. Enjoy my life with him. Just because I was in love didn't mean that I was in a coma. My life was moving forward with momentum. He let me soften because I knew I was loved, but I still kept the momentum of growing and stretching in my own life. Relationships can do that; you stop doing stuff for yourself if you are not careful. Sarah made sure that I continued going to meditation classes, and her ultimate coup was when she got me to go to a workshop on *A Course in Miracles*. Leave it to Toad to not only find the book but to come up with a group of people meeting in the most unlikely of places who wanted to share it.

Every Wednesday night, she took me to a church that met in the center of a typical California strip mall. You'd never find it if you were looking for it; it didn't have a cross or religious emblem on the outside of the building, and it was awkwardly tucked behind a New Age bookstore. The church's three rooms were once office space. This oddball location was where *A Course in Miracles* held its classes.

In the center makeshift room, there were strange people who sat on folding chairs in a circle, and all read from matching blue books. My first thought was *Get me out of here*, but then I began to relax. The words spoken at the class softened my heart, and slowly, these people lost their strangeness, and I began to accept them and actually like them, a little.

We read from the books and shared our experiences of self-discovery and somehow, magical things began to happen in our lives. Not like the magical things a fairy godmother grants you but subtle, soft shifts within us that made the world easier to be in. I began to look around me and see things differently, not just because I was in love, but because I was getting in tune and staying present in the moment.

I began to open up and give in to my intuition. I heard a strong voice inside that said do something with my life—now.

It was that same feeling that I had from work that made me feel like I should be doing something different to make the world a better place. It continued to nag and whisper until the day Sarah made me do something about it. Sarah's deep yearning to help serve the world was fulfilled by reading to children with AIDS. It was in the hematology wing in Children's Hospital, off the 805 freeway.

Hospitals are one of the few things that never bothered me; actually, they're rather remarkable. I mean, it's life or death every minute, like my office, but hospitals mean it, making them real, and my office not. Toad dragged me with her—not by choice, I might add.

It wasn't like she just brought me along and I could watch. No, that would be too easy. She had the gall to make me go through a major certification process with her—special courses in child development and psychology, a class on AIDS, the hospital rules, regulations, and procedures. It took forever, and she was ruthless.

I was a wreck the first day, anxious and nervous. I didn't want to come off as a doofus or worse, stiff. I wanted to be natural and likeable. But working with children with AIDS scared me. I wanted the kids to think I was cool. But more importantly, I didn't want to cry when I saw them. I didn't want them to think I felt sorry for them.

The kids called me Pumpernickel, leaving out the Rye. Wednesday nights or Saturdays were the days I came in tow, with Sarah's worn canvas tote bag with red straps. Inside were our favorites, all the Dr. Seuss books, *Curious George*, *Toot and Puddle*, *Goodnight Moon*, a few baby picture books, the Tolkien and *Narnia* series, and of course, *Harry Potter*.

Not everyone wanted to be read to. It took time for them to warm up to me. For some, it was within a second, and for others, it was a longer process. They were so brave; I felt small in their presence. Soon it was easy to see past the tubes and machines and see them for who they were; my worries faded.

These children were amazing and taught me that giving and receiving are the same.

"Hey, Pumpernickel," said a raspy voice owned by a boy named Trevor.

"Hey, Trev, what are we reading today?"

"Could you just hold my hand?"

"Sure."

Trevor was in the advanced stages and so thin, he was almost corpse-like. I was afraid his tiny wrist would break in my hand with the slightest touch. He taught me better. His sober green eyes were sad right then, but knowing him was a lesson in invincible strength and courage. I stroked his perfect earlobes and the patches of soft brown hair on his head.

"She didn't show up again today," he said, looking away. He was referring to his mother, a crack addict.

"I know, angel."

He was five and looked barely older than three. A tiny tear rolled down his check. "She never comes." I wanted to cry, too, but knew better.

"She does when she can."

I stayed, holding his hand and stroking his head, until he finally said, "So, what are we reading tonight?"

Trevor made it effortless for me to read aloud. His little body leaned into mine, so light, and frail, I was worried I'd crush him. He looked at me as if I were special; his love softened all my hard edges. Hearing my own voice read aloud made me slip back to the time when I read aloud in the *special* room without windows—the childhood days when I felt ashamed and dumb. Now, reading was a gift—one I was getting as much as giving.

I was selfish and conceited to think I was helping him, making him feel better when he was the one helping me.

My wounds seemed so insignificant compared to his. This boy with tubes and IVs, with a missing father and an addict mother, was God in the tiniest package. He made it possible for me to forgive my father, the special reading classes, and all the other small wounds I had carried for so long.

No one could see my heart heal but me. From the outside, it looked like nothing was different. But it was about the inside—it's always about the inside.

Chapter Twenty-Nine

"I see all things as I would have them be."

With Gordon I felt like I belonged. Butterflies of joy spun through me, my body floated to the heavens, and clouds embraced my head. To slow down time and capture my moments of sheer bliss, I wrote everything in a yellow-and-blue fabric journal. I wanted to record these electric love feelings, knowing that love changes over time. It was my way of savoring, holding on to, and gathering some type of evidence that what I was feeling was real and good.

It started with the first date. He was dressed in comfortable workout attire that, without trying or meaning to, showed his trim physique. Gordon's ease with himself made me comfortable. No worries about tripping or feeling awkward. Everything and anything was fine. He gave me permission to try new things.

"I want to take you to the wall."

"Excuse me?"

"The rock wall, you know, rock climbing?" His eyes were full of fun.

"I've never done that!"

"Piece of cake. You can handle it."

"OK," I said, trying to convince myself.

The gym was called Rock the House. It had ten walls to choose from, depending on your ability. My wall was the one the two- and three-year-olds climbed, a gentle slope with half a dozen colorful pegs.

Gordon was Spiderman without the costume. He wasn't cocky about his athletic ability. He was quietly confident about everything. This was the difference between him and the other men in my life—not that I was comparing. Confidence is when a guy looks you in the eye instead of looking around the room. It's about asking questions instead of making statements. But the best part was his ability to laugh at his own mistakes and not at his own jokes.

I made it to the second wall on our first date. It was harder than I thought, not physically but mentally.

"How'd you know I'd like it?" I asked, drenched in sweat.

"Gut feel."

"Do you do this a lot?"

"Nah."

"Liar."

"OK, when I can. It's a lot more fun outside."

Gordon brought balance to my life. He worked hard and played hard. He taught me how to mountain climb, first in the gym and then at nearby state parks that I never knew existed. Sometimes, we would strap mountain bikes to the back of his car. We ended up in parks thick with forests of pine, coastal oak, and sage.

Only a half-hour out of the city, and I felt so far away. It was easy to slow down.

Having arrived at one of the parks, we quickly got the bikes off the car and adjusted our sneakers and fanny packs. Soon we were whizzing up and down rocky dirt paths. Gordon led the way off one of the main trails, where we discovered a hidden creek that led to a small waterfall no taller than a two-story house and two feet wide. The cascading water was seasonal, visible only after the rainy winter months. At the bottom was an oval pool of clear, cold water, where stones were visible and enticing to touch. The pool of water was framed by wildflowers in shades of pale blues, yellow, and white, and yellow daisies. The sky was blue with wispy clouds—another perfect seventy-degree day.

Gordon's movements were slow and patient. After admiring the surroundings, he bent down to pick a flower. When I stretched my entire body in one move toward the flower, my foot slid off the pedal and my hand skidded off the handlebars. I fell like a newborn chick spilling out of its nest, off of my bike with a thud. I bumped my head on the way down, which left a lump on my forehead. I lay crumpled at his feet.

He gently picked me up and said with a charming smile, "Hey, Grace, there is no need to fall at my feet. You can stand to worship."

"Did you feel that earthquake, or was it an avalanche?" I said, as I rubbed the bump that would soon turn into a purple eggplant. The flower was decapitated in my left hand. When Gordon wasn't looking, I placed it in my bra to put in my journal later.

I wasn't made for off-trail mountain biking. I was made for the stationary type back at the gym.

Back on the rocky trail that twisted and snarled, I hit a five-inch stone—a boulder to me. I fell forward on my bike so that my crotch was steering the bike and my feet dangled close to the spokes. It stung like a bee, and I prayed Gordon wouldn't look back.

He did look back and said, "I guess there's no kids in the future."

"No, really, this feels good. Try it."

"You know we can go back."

"No, no, really. I'm having a blast."

"I thought so." He waited for me to get back on my bike, and asked, "Are you really OK?" He wasn't looking at my head.

"Fine," I murmured.

He saw how mortified I was. We weren't even going fast. He tried to make me feel better by saying, "You know, I fall off all the time. You are so much better at hanging on than I am."

Sure. Right. He rode his bike like he was Lance Armstrong after his seventh Tour de France win. I gave him a thanks-for-trying smile, but I knew how pathetic I looked.

When we did make it back to the car, I wished there were a second ice pack for the bump on my head. We lay back on a patch of cut grass and looked at puffy clouds that were the shape of sheep. That's when he said, "Ryley, where've you been?"

"Here ... waiting."

"What took you so long?"

"What took *you* so long?"

We rolled into each other and kissed until the grass made our skin itch. We made it home to continue our date in the bedroom.

It wasn't just the mountains that Gordon exposed me to; it was the water, his first love. He introduced me to sailing and playing on the ocean, which soon became our favorite pastime. He loved the water so much, you'd think he was allergic to land. He uncovered a world of water that I never knew existed. We'd watch outdoor concerts and fireworks from the boat. These magical concerts rocked me softly, as the sounds and sights reflected off the bay.

In the summer and fall, he raced his boat every other Wednesday after work. When the races were over, there was always a regatta, a party outside of the yacht club. The sun was low and the sunsets vivid when the real fun began. The air was almost edible—ocean mist blended with grilled masterpieces, as live music or Jimmy Buffet played in the background. Everyone had one thing in common—a love of the water.

The weekend events were most special. Dressed in his classic style, he took my hand and led me, opening doors for me like a timeless gentleman. I loved his attention to detail. For someone who couldn't cook, he appreciated good food and stocked the boat well, often bringing a basket filled with the best fine wines and their accoutrements—aged cheeses, baguettes, and hot gourmet snacks. But the topper was the cloth napkins and matching placemats.

After the outdoor concerts or evening sails, we would dock the boat. Down below in the main salon, he'd kissed me on the mouth and then on the neck. We'd groped each other in pure high-school style. Our jeans flew off, and then he was rubbing against me under a sleeping bag. Camping out on the boat had a new meaning.

There's a lot to say about good sex—he's a keeper, for starters.

His love washed over me like the blankets he wrapped me in to keep me warm. When I looked into his face, it was warm and gentle; the edges were soft and fuzzy, as if I couldn't see his outline. I felt the inside of him—yummy, like liquid love oozing all over my body, warming my soul. He saw me, he got me, he knew me. He identified parts of myself that I didn't recognize or know. He enveloped me with a deep understanding and knowingness.

Chapter Thirty

"When I am healed I am not healed alone."

Gordon was perfect.

But also human. Human, with a few major human flaws. Don't get me wrong—I loved him but hated that we had exactly opposite views in politics. He stood for the donkey or the elephant; I forget which one is which. Whatever—he was the other animal and it drove me nuts. He was a Republican. We couldn't talk politics or watch the primaries together without going crazy or getting into a heated debate. But also, there were those other things, like his not being tall and the fact that I made more money than he did.

I tried to get over it and focus on the big picture, focus on the day-to-day good. Like when Gordon took me sailing on his boat for the first time on another warm summer day. It was early in the double digits of our dates. I think it was number twenty-one. You'd think after all the times I'd sailed with Toad, it would have rubbed off—knowing something, anything, about the sport. Not. He asked if I'd sailed before, and I told him yes. I'm sure he thought I was a liar. The boat floated out of the slip effortlessly, effortlessly to me because Gordon was doing all the work, while I was in the way, trying to be helpful. He finally asked me in the most patient and kindest of tones, "Why don't you relax and have a seat?" His eyes pointed to a cushioned seat by the wheel.

"Oh, I can be your bow mate" was the first bit of incorrect terminology that he ignored.

I'm sure it was the last place he wanted me, but being the perfect gentleman, he just smiled and offered, "OK, how about port side?" I immediately went to the right side. Did he roll his eyes at my error? Did he correct me? No, he pretended I was on the port side.

The water sparkled, as seagulls seemed to call to one another, "There's a dumb ass on this boat. Watch her, fellas." I took in the ocean breeze and the cloudless day and closed my eyes for a moment of bliss. The water slapped on the side of the boat and with each wave, my body relaxed. I stood up to look at the view before us; we were leaving the bay, and the sight of day sailors, blue water, and flawless sky, topped with a perfect breeze, was glorious.

Gordon said, "Helm's alee."

I smiled back to him to say OK to whatever that meant. And then, in a flash, the boom hit me and I was overboard. The water was so icy cold, the weight of my clothes so heavy, I thought I would drown. But before I could gasp and grasp for a breath, Gordon scooped me onto the deck.

"What happened?" I asked, my hair plastered to my face, shirt soaked around my neck, bra exposed—I looked like a losing contestant in a wet T-shirt contest. Gordon covered me up, swept my hair out of my face with his forefinger, and said, "Well, Grace, looks like you got sailing confused with snorkeling."

I was mortified, looking like a drowned rat with my klutz mode in full gear; I wanted to cry. I looked at Gordon with welled-up eyes, embarrassed and humiliated, as he waited patiently. In that moment, something remarkable happened. It was as if time stood still to let something be revealed.

There was no breeze or sound, as if I could hear a single

blade of grass move. He looked at me with his soft eyes and smiled with one corner of his mouth. I looked back and wanted to say, "I feel so stupid in this body." I wanted to say it because I felt so heavy and clumsy. It was hard to move, let alone look sexy, in my drenched outfit, with the extra padding that I still hadn't lost since I met him. As I began to shape the words, he interrupted me, slowly put a finger to my lips, and said, "I know how you feel. But don't. You are so beautiful." His voice was calm and distinctive.

Dumbfounded, I stared at him; my eyes went funny and noticed the edges of his body were translucent and glowing, as if he weren't real, as if he weren't there. But he was there, and he read my mind. And in that moment, I felt as if I had gone home.

I never told him that he read my mind; my tongue was too heavy to lift the words. I stood there for what felt like days and knew I would remember that moment.

Gordon was one of the rare few who wasn't afraid of my being strong. Men can get turned off when they find out you're making more money than they are or have the corner office. He liked my success and wasn't competitive because he was successful too. He was strong in himself, present, not playing a role, and I liked that—loved it, in fact.

But the best of all, he listened to me, really listened. He heard and watched things that I said and did and took special note of them. For instance, when we were outside—biking, hiking, climbing, or just in nature—he noticed that I like to pick up acorns. My favorites were the light chestnut-colored ones with their hats still on. I never said anything when I picked them up; it was just an automatic reflex.

On my first birthday that we celebrated together, he presented me with a gift in a black velvet box the size of my palm. Inside was an 18-karat-gold necklace with three acorns adorned in jewels. The first thing he said when pointing to each acorn was, "One is for you. One is for us. And one is for our future."

"How did you know I love acorns?"

"Lucky guess," he said, blushing.

The months flew by and after almost two years, Sarah finally got it—this was a relationship that could last.

The long-awaited novena prayed so many years before actually came true. There was a God, and this was how he showed his bona fide existence—in giving a gift beyond my wildest dream. I'd finally learned that relationships weren't perfect, but this came pretty damn close.

The best part was the trust, a trust and conviction based on never cheating. It was more than a verbal commitment— we had each felt the pain of someone's cheating on us, which gave us the platform for a vow to never do it to each other. Why would anyone hurt the person he or she loved? And cheating hurts. We couldn't do it, not even if the other never found out. Love can't last without trust.

On a December night close to Christmas, he had a special surprise. The nights had become cooler as the days grew shorter. When Gordon showed up at my home, he was acting strange. He asked me three times to make sure I dressed warmly.

"You ready?" was the first thing he said as he walked through the door.

"Well, hello, nice to see you, too. What's the rush?"

"No rush. Let's go."

He moved me swiftly out of the house and zoomed to an elegant hotel on the bay, which had a small and tidy marina behind it. Waiting at the dock for us was a black gondola; in it, was a man wearing a straw hat with a red ribbon, just like in Italy.

My jaw dropped.

"What's this?" I asked slowly. He gave me a flushed smile. That's when I knew something was up.

It was a clear and crisp night. The black sky was flawless, a night to see a shooting star. Gordon took my elbow, helping me into the teetering gondola—he knew me well, so he held on tight. Once we settled into our seat, a cashmere blanket was placed over our legs.

The man with the hat paddled the gondola gently and effortlessly. We took in the night with only the sound of his oar dipping into the water. The stars reflected brightly on the flat water. We were taken to a restaurant not too far away. As we approached, the smell of garlic drifted in the air. On the small dock, waiting to greet us, was a round man dressed in a tuxedo; he was playing Bach on his violin. Gordon smiled, as if everything were going off without a hitch. I was speechless.

Our personal violinist followed us to an intimate table in the corner of the restaurant. I felt like I was floating; the candlelight and romance did that, made my movements fluid and dance-like. Dinner was French and perfect. Dessert was even better—a four-tiered masterpiece laced in edible flowers and chocolate.

The magic didn't end after dinner or when the gondola brought us back. It was still going strong when we arrived back at his condominium, where a fire sparked to life with a single match. Soon, glowing flames illuminated the living room. The burning wood cracked and blazed. Three small votive candles were lit on top of the mantel, making the wall behind them golden. As Chopin played in the background, Gordon handed me a glass of champagne.

After taking a first sip, he took my hand, almost trembling and looked into my eyes. In a shaky voice, he said, "You are my everything. I love you so much. Thank you for opening my heart and giving me a world I would have never known. Please … I want to spend the rest of my life with you. Will you marry me?"

My heart grew wings and lifted to the night, as tears rolled down my face.

The first person I told was Sarah.

"Well, it's about time!"

"Weren't you the one who said we were going too fast?"

"Yeah, but that was two years ago. Tell me all the details."

I told her about the boat and what he'd said. I told her everything I felt and then asked, "Yeah, what about you and the *Rock-a-fella*?"

"Living together suits me fine. You get married first and tell me how it goes." She paused. "I have to say, Rye, you've got it together. I mean, you really seem happy in your own skin, and it's not about Gordon. It's about you."

"I think you might be right."

"So what are the plans?"

"You know that small, one-room cobblestone church on the ocean in Marblehead, Massachusetts? That's what I want—and a tiny reception, simple and beautiful."

"No big wedding?"

"I'm over the Cinderella thing. I want it to be intimate."

"Like it."

"Will you be my maid of honor?"

"What about your sister?"

"Well, I was hoping maybe both of you could be it. Is that too lame?"

"Not unless we have to share the same dress."

When the wedding time came I was surprisingly calm, maybe because it was such a small wedding or maybe because it was so simple. Or maybe because when things are meant to be, they become easy. Don't get me wrong: I was nervous before walking down the aisle and worried that the dress didn't fit, but it did and everything was as close to perfect as things on earth can be. I was loved and supported and so happy.

I was married.

I didn't know what to expect. It was better than I imagined. There was this low, rumbling feeling of security that grounded everything that I did. I couldn't believe I would have felt so changed. It's not like I didn't spend every minute for more than a year with Gordon. This was distinctly different. Grounded. Secure. No, I think it had to do more with being connected; whatever—it was good.

On the second night of our honeymoon, we were settled into our bed, fooling around. I peeked over at his left hand to look at his new, shiny wedding band. The gold band pulled at my heart. It was spectacular, gorgeous—because he belonged to me and only me.

This was the ring I had fantasized about as a kid. His on his finger, mine on mine. When I was in high school, I'd take my signet ring, place it on my ring finger, and twist it around, exposing the bare gold band. It looked like a wedding band, and I pretended it was real. Now it was strange and amazing to have the real one. I couldn't keep my eyes off of it. Love worked its way through my throat to my heart and spread through every fiber of my being, opening me up, making me still. Who would have thought a piece of jewelry could do so much?

Chapter Thirty-One

*"Forgiveness is the key to happiness. The unforgiving
mind is in despair, without the prospect of a future,
which can offer anything but more despair."*

A month later, I was back in the full weave of work.
Everyone could tell I was married because my office was
covered in wedding pictures—some in frames, some not.

A never-ending stream of phone calls, along with business
plans and projections to be reviewed, kept me moving at
full throttle. Business was up, but crazy, and the hours
swooshed by. Two o'clock would often come without lunch;
too much to do, too little time.

The phone was cradled against my ear, while I typed out
e-mails, and when I looked up for a second, there he was.

Hank.

He was standing in the door of my office with our real
estate manager. I had forgotten we needed to make a decision on new office space; we were bursting at the seams,
and our lease was up in less than eight months. Steve, my
boss, had been in New York so much that he was a part-
time resident. Even though our expenditure capital sat in
the budget that I oversaw, he usually liked to have the final
blessing on new buildings. But this time, he gave me that
decision. I wished he hadn't.

My cheeks flushed. What the hell was Hank doing here,

and how did he get into my office without someone letting me know? I was in shock, to say the least.

While I finished the conversation on the phone, I surreptitiously looked at my reflection in the window to see how cool and collected I looked. I was fine.

"Ryley, you didn't forget our two o'clock appointment?" said Janet, our company's real estate manager. At that moment, I hated her.

"Hi, Ryley," Hank said in his opulent voice and added a smile that still just about knocked me out cold.

I took in a slow breath through my nose and said, "Hi. You know, I hate to do this ... could we reschedule?" I stammered, trying not to sound forced or rude.

"You know we are running out of time," Janet said. God how I hated her.

"OK, then leave the information," I said, with a face that said, "Sorry I can't help you right now; I'll get back to you later." I needed them to go so I could gather myself.

There was a third person with them, tucked behind Hank. He was the commercial broker. He stepped forward and made a small gesture to introduce Hank. "Hank tells me you have worked together before; I just dropped by to reintroduce you. I'll follow up later."

Then he and Janet left, and Hank stayed behind.

His face was red, it was obvious that he wasn't relaxed either. I was starved and edgy.

He stepped forward. "So. How are you?" he said in a warm, adoring voice. The old feelings were so big in the remembering of him and the way we use to be. I didn't want to face those feelings or be with them. I was over this. It was as if our lives were a million years ago. But it felt like yesterday at the same time, as if one foot stepped into the present and the past swirled all into the same time—

confusing. I wasn't sure what was inside me. I had moved on, with thoughts of him erased from my head. But he still came back. When was I going to be done with all of this? With him?

I wanted to say "Busy," but instead, I blurted out, "Fine."

"Ryley, I meant to call you first, but I was afraid you wouldn't see me."

Good assumption, I thought. "What are you doing here?"

I felt naked in my office, exposed and not ready for this visit from nowhere.

"Well, I moved here a month ago and landed a job with Commercial Brokers. When I heard you were the decision maker on the new building we have, I told them we worked together in New York. They said they needed help, so here I am. So, how are you?"

"Well, I'm really buried … You know, I'm sorry for wasting your time and having to tell you … the truth is, we already made our decision to go with another building." Pause. Pause. I stood up slowly. "You know, I'm actually on the way out."

I came around my desk and headed toward the door. Hank touched my elbow as I passed him. "Could we talk? I haven't seen you in so long. Can we catch up?"

I stepped out of his grasp.

"Ryley, you should at least consider the property. It's a great building, and they have a hell of a deal worked out. Please don't let me interfere with that." He was flushed, crimson, and nervous. Really nervous.

He made me so mad, I wanted to scream. How could he invade my life like this and shake my belief of who I thought I was … am? I wanted Hank gone.

I wondered what a commission on a fifty-million-dollar

building was. Don't ask me why, but I was disgusted that he'd make some kind of commission off me and my decision. God, I wanted nothing to do with him.

"Ryley ..."

"I'm really sorry. We've made our decision," I said, pointing the lobby out to him with my eyes. And then my eyes slowly dropped, and I noticed he was wearing his wedding ring.

Why could he still get a reaction out of me? Maybe because I was so hungry. Why was he interrupting my life? My blood was starting to boil and my nerves were raw from caffeine. I'm surprised he made it out of my office in one piece without a bite or scratch marks.

Hank weighed on my mind for the rest of the day.

I did review the real estate options closely. Hank's deal was pretty good, clearly under my budget. My first choice was right at budget and a much better location. Either way, procurement would be happy. But I knew my first choice would be a better investment and better for our customers.

Hank called back and left messages. He was ready to beg for the business.

I had no respect for a cheating man. If he could cheat on his wife, what else did he cheat on?

I was married now and had something I could not possibly have imagined when I wasn't. Marriage is sacred. I would not and could not ever hurt Gordon. I loved him too much. How could Hank hurt his wife the way he did? She was no longer the bad guy—he was. Elizabett had no idea what he did before or after they were married. I was sick with myself for having had something to do with it.

Hank could have moved anywhere on the planet. Why, why did he not only choose my state, my city, my town, but also—and more importantly—how did he find out where I worked and what decisions I made? Fate? Destiny? Stalking? What the hell was he thinking?

I was raging with vengeful thoughts; I wanted to get back at him for his cruel infidelities and for stringing me along.

As I sat in my office, staring out the window and twirling a gold pen between my nose and upper lip, I let my mind plot. I sank into my large leather chair, like a baseball sinking into a worn mitt.

I let my fantasies wander; I imagined schemes I wanted to act out. Like making him get on his hands and knees in order to sign his contract, with the condition that he would bring his wife into my office and confess his infidelities. He would have to beg for her forgiveness, explaining to her what a rotten wretch he was. Yeah, he would have to come clean.

As I considered my former lover's demise, something shimmered off the left corner of my desk. Gold block letters from the bookcase were reflecting the sun. They were the letters from the spine of *A Course in Miracles.* I strolled over to pick up the familiar paperback and leafed through the pages until I felt I needed to stop.

Out popped the words *Forgiveness is the key to happiness. The unforgiving mind is in despair, without the prospect of a future which can offer anything but more despair.*

I slowly closed the book and placed it back on the shelf. I had read all I needed to. I stopped, paused, and slowly looked around my office. I could forgive Hank and I could let him go.

I looked at him in my mind's eye, as if he were standing in front of me. I saw his face and his eyes, and I realized that in some way, he was going through his life as best as he could, and in the center he was good. I was clear with myself

that I wanted to move on. I knew what love without condi-
tions was and what being faithful was. Gordon was my
present, my future. Hank was my past. I deserved love
without strings, and I'd found it, and so had Hank.

I signed the contract with the other commercial real estate
broker. Hank called the next day, and I told him the contracts
were signed, and I wished him well in his new job. I hung up.

A few weeks later, when I'd driven out to get some lunch
and just as I was parking, I ran into him again. I was moving
slowly out of my car, taking in a moment for myself outside
of the office, when I turned and saw him in the parking lot.
Oh, God no! There he was, and my first reaction was quick,
duck, dodge him. I was done with the contract; I was done
with him. Just as I was crouching down behind my car, he
saw me. It was too late; he was looking right at me, calling
out, "Ryley!" It was like a command, his arms scooping air
for me to come over. Busted. "Ryley!" he called again. "Come
on over. There's someone I want you to meet."

I stood up and walked toward his car. He was standing by
the open passenger door, holding it open to show me who
was inside. I dreaded the thought of who it could be. I was
swallowed up in that familiar vortex of feelings from the
past. But as I got closer, I saw it wasn't his wife or new
mistress; it was a tiny blonde-haired baby tucked in his car
seat. Hank unbuckled the small child and raised him for me
to see, proudly beaming like an over-ripe papa. He couldn't
do that so easily, just move on, or could he? Could I? He was
leading me into his world that was without me, leaving me
behind for good.

"This is Jake," he said to me, smiling at his chubby-faced,
tow-headed toddler. I used to wonder what Hank would
have been like as a dad. A good one.

"Hi there, Jake," I said, as I lightly touched his right foot, part of me wishing he were mine, the other part glad he was only his. And then I looked at Hank. "Yeah, we have another on the way. Can you believe it? Me, a dad?"

"Yes, I can, and it fits you quite well. He's beautiful, Hank, congratulations." And then in a blink of an eye, it was over. Hank put little Jake back in the car and drove away, as I waved to both, thinking no hard feelings. In that moment I was happy for him, happy for me. Glad to catch this glimpse of goodness in his life, as we both let go and moved on.

Back in the office, my sandwich still in the brown bag and me sitting behind my desk, I could see that little boy again in my mind's eye. Beautiful, like his dad.

My mind drifted off into a mystical daze, searching outside my window, not really gazing at anything in particular. What was that song? What was that song? I knew it and then I heard it. But didn't remember why or how. I could only hear pieces and fragments, unable to make out the singer, the writer, or band. What was that song?

It was coming from a radio playing outside my office. A familiar tune drifted through my doorway. I could barely make out the words—Bryan Ferry.

Oh baby, don't leave me here
With a low whisper
Windswept in the air.
You say it's nothing
But a game we played.
Oh, I'm feeling swept away

I thought of Hank and how much I once loved him and how complete and perfect life now was without him. I looked around my office, taking in the pictures of Sarah, of my father and sister, and finally, of Gordon. I knew beyond a doubt that I had moved beyond "what if" to what *is*. And what is was all I wanted or needed. My heart swelled with love, and I smiled.

TAYLOR G. WILSHIRE

T H E   W H A T - I F   G U Y